The Girl Who Couldn't Remember

"I love it here," George announced.

"I can't wait to get started on my tan," Bess said.

Just then something banged against the cabin door.

"What was that?" Nancy asked with a frown as she headed for the front door. She pulled it open and looked outside. "There's no one there," she said to her friends.

Nancy glanced outside again. This time she looked down—and gasped.

"What is it, Nan?" George called.

Nancy stepped aside so the others could see.

The body of a young woman was lying across the threshold!

Nancy Drew
Mystery Stories

Available from MINSTREL Books

NANCY DREW MYSTERY STORIES®

91

NANCY DREW®

THE GIRL WHO COULDN'T REMEMBER

CAROLYN KEENE

A
MINSTREL®
BOOK

PUBLISHED BY POCKET BOOKS

New York   London   Toronto   Sydney   Tokyo   Singapore

This novel is a work of fiction. Names, characters, places and incidents are either the product of the author's imagination or are used fictitiously. Any resemblance to actual events or locales or persons, living or dead, is entirely coincidental.

A MINSTREL PAPERBACK *ORIGINAL*

A Minstrel Book published by
POCKET BOOKS, a division of Simon & Schuster Inc.
1230 Avenue of the Americas, New York, NY 10020

ISBN: 0-671-66316-X

First Minstrel Books printing October 1989

10 9 8 7 6 5 4 3 2

Contents

1

Mystery Girl

"Absolutely no mysteries this time," Bess Marvin said to her friend Nancy Drew. "You promised!"

Eighteen-year-old Nancy laughed. She glanced in the rearview mirror to smile at Bess, who was sitting in the backseat of Nancy's blue sports car. Nancy, Bess, and their friend George Fayne had finally found the time to take a vacation together. Bess didn't want it interrupted.

Nancy pushed a lock of reddish blond hair off her forehead and straightened up in her seat.

1

"I do solemnly swear," she said. "For ten days I will seek out no mysteries and look for no crimes."

"Finally, a chance to relax!" George, who was Bess's cousin, stretched in the front seat beside Nancy. "We're going to have a great time."

"And get some great tans," Bess said in her most theatrical voice. "As we sun on the shores of lovely Lake Minosha in beautiful northern Wisconsin."

The three friends had been planning this trip for months. They were going to a part of Wisconsin that was famous for its unspoiled, natural beauty.

"Sounds like you've memorized the tourist brochures, Bess," Nancy said with a chuckle.

"You bet," said Bess. "But I'm glad we won't be *too* far from civilization. The town of Minosha sounds wonderful. There are all kinds of cafés and restaurants and shops, and even a theater."

"Hold it," George said. "The cabin we rented is eight miles from town, Bess. It's in the middle of the woods. We'll be too busy swimming and canoeing and hiking to shop."

Although they were cousins, George and Bess were as different as night and day. Tall and slim, George had short, curly, dark hair and

2

dark eyes. She loved sports of all kinds. Bess, slightly on the plump side, had long blond hair and blue eyes, and her favorite pastimes were shopping, eating—and going on diets.

"You'd both make great travel agents," Nancy broke in. "But let's get to Minosha first. How much farther is it, George?"

George unfolded a large map and spread it over her knees. Bess leaned forward and peered over her cousin's shoulder.

George studied the map. "Well, if my directions are perfect, we should be there in about twenty minutes."

"Maybe we could stop at a restaurant in town," Bess suggested.

"No way!" her cousin scoffed. "There's enough food in the picnic basket for an army. Plus the five bags of taco chips you bought, remember?"

"Mmm, thanks for reminding me." Bess hunted for the chips. "I'll open a bag now."

As the girls nibbled chips and chatted they gazed at the rolling green hills, neatly plowed fields, and grassy meadows outside. Then they passed a scattering of houses.

"We must be near Minosha," Nancy said.

George checked the map again. "This road will take us through town. Eight miles farther we'll find Aladdin's Cabins."

The girls reached Minosha, and the road grew more crowded. Traffic moved slowly.

"This must be a popular vacation spot," Nancy said. The car inched down the crowded street. "I hadn't expected so many cars."

"Well, at least we get a chance to see the place," Bess said. "There are some great-looking shops—hey, stop a minute, Nancy. Did you see the white dress in that window? I've got to have it."

"Bess, why do you need a new dress? We're spending ten days in the middle of the woods," George protested.

"It's smart to be prepared," Bess answered. "You never know who might come knocking at our cabin door."

"Anyone in those woods will be glad to see you—no matter what you're wearing," George said. "Nancy, let's get to the cabin as fast as we can. If Bess even sets foot in one of those shops, we may never see her again."

"Oh, you're no fun." Bess pretended to sulk. Then she suddenly bounced up in her seat. "Hey, look at that, guys!" She pointed to a long building at one end of a big parking lot. "That must be the town theater. And look what's playing."

The marquee above the wide red doors read:

4

Castle Community Theater Presents *Born Tomorrow*.

"Remember that, Nancy?" George asked.

"How could I forget?" Nancy said. "Our senior class play. Of course, we all had pretty small parts."

Bess sighed. "I only had two lines."

"Me, too," said Nancy. "But those two lines convinced me I'd better stick to detective work."

Nancy increased the car's speed as they reached the edge of town. "We're back in the wilds now," she commented. "Goodbye town, hello sun and fun."

A few miles farther on they turned off the highway. They began to follow a narrow road banked on both sides by thick forest. Above the trees, the sky was clear blue, and the sun shone brightly.

"It's beautiful," George said. She gave a contented sigh.

Nancy slowed the car. A freshly tarred section of road ahead had been set off with cone-shaped markers. Nancy steered carefully around them. She caught sight of a small sign nearly hidden behind a marker. On it was a picture of a lamp with a genie in swimming trunks rising out of it. Below the picture were the words Aladdin's Cabins—1/4 Mile.

"Almost there." Nancy made a sharp left turn onto a dirt road.

A small wood cabin at the end of the road had the word *OFFICE* painted in yellow letters above its screen door. The girls climbed out of the car and walked to the door.

"Come in," a man's voice called when Nancy knocked.

The office was tiny—nothing more than a desk, a wastebasket, and a fabulous view of the lake through the room's only window. Behind the desk sat a man about forty years old with thinning blond hair.

"We've rented a cabin," Nancy said. "The reservation is in the name of Nancy Drew."

"Right." The man glanced at the register on his desk, then stood up and held out his hand. "I'm Bob Wickman, owner of Aladdin's Cabins. Welcome!"

The girls signed the register, and Mr. Wickman led them down a path through the woods.

"You can leave your car by the office," he explained. "It's just a short walk to the cabins. Each cabin has a separate trail that branches off from the main path. You'll have plenty of privacy."

Nancy breathed in the forest fragrance deeply. "It smells wonderful," she said.

6

"Yep," agreed Mr. Wickman. "The air's great here—really clean. And you could drink straight from the lake if you wanted. We're lucky. Here's your trail," he added.

At the end of the trail was a cabin with a whitewashed front porch. Like Mr. Wickman's office, the cabin was small. But the trees overhead gave it all the natural beauty the girls could have hoped for.

"This is great." George flashed a wide grin. Nancy and Bess nodded enthusiastically.

"I'm glad you like it," said Mr. Wickman. "I built all the cabins myself. My grandfather from Sweden taught me how. Let me show you around."

The cabin was furnished simply but comfortably. In the main room there were two sofa beds, small pine side tables, and a large, hand-carved pine table with four chairs. A big stone fireplace was set into one wall.

Kitchen appliances and a wall phone were arranged along the opposite wall. At the back of the cabin were the bathroom and a small bedroom with two simple wooden beds. The fresh smell of evergreen trees came through the open windows.

"It's perfect," Nancy said. "Did you make the furniture, too?"

Mr. Wickman smiled. "Most of it. Now I'll show you our dock."

A path led from the back of the cabin to the lake and dock. Two ducks were paddling in the water. From far in the distance a loon called.

The girls gazed, spellbound, out over the sparkling water. The surface of the lake was dotted by three small islands. The opposite shore was thick with trees.

Mr. Wickman broke the silence. "Well, you're all set." He handed Nancy the key to the cabin. "There are two sailboats, a motorboat, a rowboat, and some canoes by the main dock near the office. You're welcome to use them. Just pick up the motorboat keys or paddles or oars in the office. And have fun!" He gave them a cheery wave and set off for his office.

"Let's hurry and unpack," Nancy said.

When the suitcases had been put away, they hesitated. Boating or swimming—which would it be?

"Let's take out a sailboat," Bess finally said. "But you guys had better do the sailing. I haven't had much practice since day camp."

Nancy and George agreed. The girls hurried to one of the sailboats. Bess hopped on while Nancy and George pushed the boat into deep water. Then they too climbed aboard.

"Is this great, or is this great?" George sighed happily as they sped along.

"I'd say it's perfect," Nancy answered.

She let out the sail. For the next half hour, the boat rocked gently in a light breeze. They passed a few canoes and two Windsurfers. The other sailors waved and called out friendly greetings.

Finally Bess sat up. "I hate to break the spell," she said. "But I'll wither away if we don't get lunch. It's after two o'clock!"

Nancy and George agreed that they were hungry, too, and they headed the sailboat toward shore.

Back in the cabin the girls made a quick salad and grilled cheese sandwiches. After eating, they shared dishwashing duty.

"I love it out here," Nancy announced.

"Me, too," Bess agreed. She scraped salad off a plate and then handed the plate to George. "And the best part is, not one dangerous thing can happen. I can finally start that juicy book I'm dying to read."

"And I can start a nice, dark tan." George rinsed the plate and passed it to Nancy to dry. "And then I want to try—"

Just then something banged against the cabin door.

Nancy almost dropped the dish she was drying. "What was that?" she asked with a frown.

"Visitors!" Bess exclaimed. "I knew I should have bought that white dress in town."

Nancy laughed as she headed for the front door. She pulled it open and looked outside. "There's no one there," she said to her friends.

"That's odd," George said, as Nancy glanced outside again. This time, she looked down—and gasped.

"What is it, Nan?"

Nancy took a deep breath. "Sorry, Bess . . . George," she answered. "But I didn't go looking for this mystery." She stepped aside so the others could see.

The body of a young woman was lying across the threshold.

2

A Blank Wall

Quickly Nancy bent down to find the girl's wrist.

After a long moment she announced, "Her pulse is okay."

As Nancy spoke, the girl moaned and tried to sit up. Her face was bruised and covered with scratches.

Nancy knelt beside her. "Please hold still for a minute," she said. "You've been hurt. I don't know how badly."

"Should we move her into the cabin?" George asked.

"Better not," Nancy answered. "Not yet, anyway. If she hurt her back, moving her might

11

be very dangerous. I'll just check to make sure she doesn't have any broken bones."

There weren't any broken bones, but the girl's face, arms, and hands were bruised and scratched. The hem of her pink polo shirt was torn, and some of the fabric was missing. Nancy found traces of blood under the girl's fingernails. There was a nasty swelling just above her right temple.

The young woman seemed about Nancy's age—eighteen or nineteen. She had high cheekbones and curly auburn hair. The girl's eyes fluttered open. They were large dark eyes—eyes that looked frightened. Yet despite her fear and bruises, the girl was beautiful.

Nancy helped her to her feet, then guided her to one of the sofa beds in the living room.

"Can you tell us what happened?" Nancy asked.

The young woman hesitated. She shook her head.

"I can't . . . I can't remember anything. There were the woods . . . I was trying to get out!"

Her eyes filled with tears.

"Bess, get some ice for the bump on her head," Nancy ordered. "And a glass of water."

Bess hurried to the refrigerator. Nancy patted the girl's hand to comfort her.

12

"Can you tell us your name?" she asked.

The girl nodded vaguely. "Toby . . . Toby Jackson," she said finally. "At least I can remember that."

"What hurts the most?" Nancy asked.

"J-just my head," Toby whispered. She cleared her throat and spoke more firmly. "Everything else feels banged up but pretty much okay."

"Can you remember anything besides your name?" Nancy asked. "How about where you live?"

A bewildered expression came over Toby's face. "My mind is a blank," she said.

Her eyes filled with tears again, but she brushed them away and smiled faintly. "I'm not usually this scatterbrained. At least, I hope not."

Nancy frowned. "It looks to me as though whatever gave you that bump on your head caused partial amnesia."

"Amnesia?" Bess asked. "You mean she can't remember anything?"

"Right," said Nancy. "Sometimes a head injury will do that to people. It almost always goes away pretty quickly." She frowned at Toby's panicky expression. "I think we'd better get you to a hospital. And call the police."

"No!" Toby cried. "Don't! Please!" She tried

to stand up but collapsed weakly back onto the sofa. "Please don't go to the police. I'm frightened! I don't know why, but I—I'm afraid I've done something wrong!" Her eyes brimmed over with tears.

"Hold it," Nancy said gently. "No one's trying to frighten you. I'm just worried about the bump on your head."

Toby looked desperate—and desperately confused. "I wish I could remember what happened," she said. "I know I'm not a criminal. But I also know I can't face the police. Please don't turn me in!"

Nancy stared at Toby. She had no idea what to do. Something about Toby made Nancy want to help her. But why was Toby so afraid of the police? Could she be guilty of some crime?

Toby saw the doubt in Nancy's face. She reached forward and grabbed Nancy's hand.

"What if this had happened to you?" she whispered. "What if you couldn't remember anything? What if you thought you might be in danger? What would you do?"

Nancy looked into Toby's eyes again and made up her mind. Whatever Toby might have done, Nancy believed she was no criminal. She was just a girl who needed help.

She glanced at her friends. They looked worried.

14

"Toby, I'm a detective," Nancy said slowly. "My name is Nancy Drew, and these are my friends Bess Marvin and George Fayne. We might be able to help figure out what happened to you. I'm willing to let you stay here, but just for a couple of days, unless your injuries start looking worse. If that's okay with my friends, that is."

Bess and George nodded. Nancy smiled gratefully at them.

"I won't tell the police where you are for forty-eight hours. We can all do some investigating," Nancy continued. "If your memory doesn't come back and we haven't found out anything by that time, I'll have to call them."

Bess rolled her eyes. "There goes the perfect vacation. But this is much more exciting," she quickly added.

Toby looked both surprised and grateful. "Thank you all!" she cried. "Amnesia—that's pretty scary. I'm lucky I landed on a detective's doorstep! I wish I could tell you more."

"Don't worry about that," Nancy said. "You need to feel better first. Would you like to take a shower?"

"That would be wonderful."

"We can lend you fresh clothes," George said, helping Toby to her feet.

Nancy frowned. "Speaking of clothes—

15

Toby, do you have any idea how your shirt got ripped? Or where you got that tar on your sandals? There's tar on the hem of your pants, too."

Toby shook her head. "That's a mystery to me, Nancy. I'm sorry."

She reached into her pants pocket and pulled out a few things. "There might be some clues here."

"Great," Nancy said. "After your shower, we'll see if they jog your memory."

Twenty minutes later Toby came out of the bathroom, looking much better. She had on Bess's flowered kimono and was dabbing antiseptic onto the scratches on her arm.

"Why don't you lie down on the sofa?" Nancy suggested. "Then I can ask you a few questions."

Toby stretched out on the sofa. Nancy picked up the things Toby had handed her earlier.

"A flyer for *Born Tomorrow*," Nancy began. "It's playing at the community theater. Were you planning to go?"

Toby thought for a moment, then shook her head. "I don't remember," she said.

"What about this?" Nancy held up a round, green button with the letters WEB printed on it. Toby shook her head.

Next Nancy showed her a scrap of paper. On

it someone had penciled several words: *wood, boat yard,* and *2:30.*

"I don't even know if that's my handwriting," Toby said with a sigh.

Nancy patted her shoulder. "Don't worry. There's just one more thing here—a telephone message."

The message read, "Toby—Call (608) 555-3535—Sandy."

Toby read the message carefully. Once more she shook her head. "Sorry, Nancy. It just doesn't ring a bell."

"Well, I can call the number," Nancy said. "That ought to tell us something."

She walked over to the wall phone and dialed the number. After several rings, someone picked up at the other end.

"Hello," Nancy said. "I'm looking for a Toby Jackson. Can you tell me where she is?"

She listened for a moment. Then she said, "There's so much noise on your end, I can barely hear. Where exactly am I calling?"

After a moment more, Nancy said, "I see. Well, thanks, anyway. 'Bye."

Nancy turned to Toby. "Does the University of Wisconsin in Madison mean anything to you?"

Toby shook her head. "No. Why?"

"This phone number," Nancy explained.

17

"It's for the student snack bar. The guy on the phone said there are thirty thousand students at the university. And we don't know which one you're supposed to be calling."

Bess sighed. "Up against a blank wall already."

But Nancy had another idea. "Maybe the college admissions office can help us," she said. "I'll get their number from information."

A few minutes later she turned back to the three other girls.

"Well, Toby, now we know a little more about you. You're registered as a student at the college. But they expected you back a week ago."

"A week ago!" Toby looked worried. "It's nice to know I have some place to go, I guess."

"We can try the university again if we need to," Nancy said. "But I've got a few other things to check out first. Like those tar stains on your clothes." She picked up Toby's pink polo shirt and examined it.

"Remember the road we drove in on?" she asked George and Bess. "There was a tarred stretch I had to drive around. It was just before we saw the sign for Aladdin's Cabins. Let's go back over there."

Nancy dug through her purse for the car

keys. "And we could check out the note that was in Toby's pocket," she said.

Bess sounded excited. "'Boat yard. Two-thirty,'" she repeated. "If Toby had an appointment there today, she missed it. But we might find something else."

"One of us should stay here with Toby," George suggested. "Why don't you two investigate? Maybe Toby and I can come up with more clues."

Toby grinned. "With my headache, I don't think I can think of any clues," she said. "But I'll try my best."

Nancy and Bess said goodbye and hurried to the car. They were quickly back at the freshly tarred area on the main road.

An empty yellow convertible sat on the side of the road not far from them. Two of the cone-shaped markers protecting the road had been knocked over.

Nancy and Bess scrambled out of Nancy's car. "There's been an accident since we were here last," Nancy said. "Look at these tire marks."

"Is this the car that crashed?" Bess hurried to the yellow convertible.

Nancy joined her. "No scratches or dents." She showed Bess a heavy, black skid mark. It

19

started in the middle of the road and curved into the tarred area.

"Whoever skidded must have knocked over those markers," Bess said.

"And then crashed." Nancy pointed to a nearby tree. A long, deep gash had been cut into the bark.

"Wow." Bess shuddered. "I wonder if anyone was hurt?"

"Toby might have been," Nancy said. "If she was driving, she could have been thrown against the windshield."

"And bumped her head!" Bess exclaimed.

Nancy nodded. "She might have been confused and wandered through the woods to our cabin."

Nancy looked around. "But the car that crashed isn't here. That might mean someone was with Toby. And that they left her to wander away."

"Maybe there's someone else hurt," Bess said. "Maybe in these woods."

"Could be," Nancy said. "We'd better look around."

They headed into the woods. There was no path, and they had to force their way through thick underbrush.

"Ouch!" Bess pushed a thorny branch out of the way. "This is slow going, Nan."

"I was thinking the same thing," Nancy replied. "Why don't we split up? We can cover more ground that way. You head toward Aladdin's Cabins. I'll check out the other direction."

"Don't go too far." Bess sounded nervous. "It's a little creepy in here."

Nancy nodded. "Don't worry."

As she struggled alone through the brush, Nancy smiled. Bess always got nervous in unfamiliar places, even when there was nothing to worry about.

Suddenly a long, piercing scream shattered the silence of the woods.

Nancy turned toward the sound.

"Bess, I'm coming!" she shouted.

3

Stranger in the Woods

"Nancy!" Bess screamed. "Where are you?"

"I'm coming!" Nancy pushed through the woods.

Tangled roots and vines tripped her. The leaves were so thick she could hardly see. But she heard Bess crashing toward her and a moment later she caught a glimpse of Bess's orange T-shirt. They met face-to-face in a clearing.

"Are you all right?" Nancy asked.

Bess nodded. "Just let me catch my breath."

After a moment she went on. "One of my shoelaces came untied. I knelt down to tie it. Someone came up behind me. I thought it was you, and I turned around. But it was a man, staring at me!"

Bess shuddered. "He grabbed my wrist. And he said, 'Where is she?' I pulled away and started screaming. He heard you shout, and he ran off toward the road."

"Come on," Nancy said. "We've got to catch him."

She dashed toward the road. Bess followed behind her.

As Nancy reached the edge of the road, she heard a car door slam. With a loud screech, the yellow convertible sped around the bend and disappeared.

"No use trying to catch him," Nancy said. Bess had joined her on the road. "He was going too fast. Did you get a good look at him?"

Bess nodded. "I'll never forget that face. He had lots of freckles and red, curly hair. About our age, or maybe a little older. Not bad-looking—but that's all I noticed. I was too frightened."

Nancy patted her friend on the shoulder. "Bess, I know you've had a bad scare," she said. "But Toby might really be in danger. I still want to check out the boat yard in Minosha. Would that be okay?"

Bess took a deep breath. "All right. Anything's better than hanging around here. I mean, what if that guy comes back?" She beat Nancy to the car.

In Minosha, Nancy pulled into a gas station to buy a map of the town. The boat yard was close by, and they were there in a few minutes. This part of town was run-down, and the streets were empty.

"What a creepy neighborhood," Bess said, sorry they'd gone there. "I didn't know Minosha had a section like this."

Large warehouses lined both sides of the street. The sidewalks were deserted, too, as if no one ever bothered to set foot in the place. In the boat yard itself there was no sign of life.

The sun threw deep shadows on the ground. The yard was huge, and the girls shivered as they walked along the hulking shadows. Big, old boats had been hauled up for repairs. Piles of raw lumber lay scattered on the ground.

Something rattled, and Nancy and Bess both jumped. But it was only a tin can being blown by the wind.

"This place is spooky," Bess whispered. She stepped carefully over a piece of lumber. "Do you think Toby's note meant she was supposed to pick up some wood here at two-thirty?"

"Maybe," Nancy answered. Then she caught sight of a woman in overalls working on a small sailboat.

24

"Finally—a person," Nancy said. She called to the woman. "Could we talk to you for a minute?"

The woman wiped the sweat off her forehead with her sleeve and nodded.

"We're looking for a girl named Toby Jackson," Nancy said. "Does that name ring a bell?"

The woman thought for a moment, then shook her head. "Never heard of her," she said. "And I'm the only one here right now. Sorry."

"Thanks, anyway," Nancy said. "We might as well go back to the car," she told Bess.

"We could come back when there are more people around," Bess said.

"Maybe tomorrow." Nancy pulled out of the parking lot. "Let's get back to the cabin for dinner. Aren't you hungry?"

"Starved." Bess sighed with relief. "I thought you'd never ask."

Nancy chuckled as she pointed the car toward Aladdin's Cabins. She was glad Bess was cracking jokes again. Nancy knew her friend had been badly scared by the stranger in the woods.

"After what you've been through," Nancy told Bess, "you deserve double helpings of everything."

25

Bess laughed. "Hey, look," she said. "There's that community theater again."

Bess peered at the theater marquee as they passed.

"And the sign says it's opening night."

"That's interesting," Nancy said. "I wonder if Toby was going tonight? She did have that brochure for the theater."

Back at Aladdin's Cabins, the girls parked the car in front of the office. They walked down the winding path to their own cabin.

"Put some food in the oven, quick." Nancy pushed open the front door.

"You're too late," George announced. "Toby and I already took care of it."

George stood at the stove, turning over four juicy hamburgers. She grinned at her friends.

Toby was setting the table. When she looked up at Nancy, her eyes were hopeful. "What did you find out?" she asked.

"Not much, I'm afraid," Nancy told her gently. "Nothing that can't wait until dinner."

"Well, then, make yourselves useful," George said. "Those carrots need scraping. And one of you can mix up some lemonade."

Ten minutes later, the girls sat down to salad, hamburgers, and corn on the cob.

"Not a bad meal," Bess said happily. "I

couldn't ask for anything more. Except chocolate cake for dessert."

"We do what we can for hardworking detectives," George teased.

"That's right," Toby said. "You all deserve a reward."

"Well, I wish we had found out more than we did." Nancy described the afternoon's adventures to Toby and George.

"What do you think, Toby?" she asked when she had finished. "Can you remember a car accident? Or a guy with red hair and a yellow convertible?"

Toby closed her eyes for a moment. When she opened them, she looked confused again. "I can almost see something," she said. "But I'm not sure. I don't know if it's in my head, or if it's just what you've told me."

"Well, keep trying," Nancy answered. "It will come back. And I want to ask you a favor."

"Anything," Toby said. "You're all being so nice!"

"I don't think you'll like this," Nancy warned. "But it could be important. I want you to come to the community theater tonight. We'll all be with you. I want you to stand near the theater when everyone is walking in. You may see someone you remember."

Toby's eyes grew huge in her pale face. "I'll try . . . but I'm frightened."

She scratched at her bruised arms. Nancy understood it was very hard for Toby to place herself in any danger.

"Don't worry. No one will hurt you," Nancy said gently. "We'll all be there to protect you. And you might recognize a friend. Remember the flyer in your pocket? Maybe you were supposed to meet someone at the play tonight. We might be able to clear up this whole mystery right away."

"I know you're right," Toby said. "But I still feel very frightened. Do you promise to stay right near me?"

"We all will," Nancy promised. Bess and George nodded.

"Okay," Toby said at last. "I'll go."

The girls cleared the table and washed the dishes. Then they changed into slacks and sweaters.

As they walked up the path, George inhaled the sweet-smelling air. "It's cold here after sunset," she remarked. Nancy could tell George was trying to cheer up Toby.

"But the cabin has a fireplace. Later tonight we can roast marshmallows."

Nancy nodded. "Great idea," she agreed. Toby looked a bit less nervous.

When the girls arrived at the theater, the parking lot was mostly empty.

"Good—we're early."

Nancy pulled into a parking place. "We can watch everyone go in."

They climbed out of the car and started toward the theater lobby. Toby gazed at the large sign over the entrance.

"Castle Community Theater," she murmured. She didn't try to hide her fear.

"What is it?" George asked. "What's wrong?"

Toby shuddered. "It—it's the sign," she said. "It scares me. But I don't know why!"

Nancy patted her on the shoulder. "Don't worry, Toby," she said. "We're all here with you." She smiled. "And we're absolutely sure that the sign can't hurt you."

Toby managed a stiff laugh. But Nancy could tell she really wanted to turn and run.

"We'll stand right under the sign, next to the main doors," Nancy directed. "That way we'll see the most people."

People were beginning to arrive. Before long, cars began to fill the parking lot and people streamed into the theater.

"What a crowd!" Bess said. "This production must be better than the one we did in high school."

George rolled her eyes. "I hope so, Bess," she said. "Otherwise they'll all ask for their money back."

"Do you recognize anyone?" Nancy asked Toby in a low voice.

Toby shook her head. Her face was strained and tired looking. "They're all strangers," she said.

The ushers began to close the theater doors. The show was about to start.

Nancy sighed. "Well, at least we tried. We might as well head back to the cabin."

Toby shook her head as they walked back to the car. "I don't know whether I'm relieved or disappointed," she said.

Just then a big blue sedan pulled into a parking space in front of them. A tall, gray-haired man got out and headed toward the theater. He caught sight of Toby and stopped short.

"You!" he exclaimed. "What are you—"

Toby gasped. She turned and ran blindly away.

"Toby!" Bess shouted. "Stop!"

"Watch out!" Nancy yelled.

Toby had bolted into the street—straight into the path of an oncoming car.

4

Hit and Miss

The driver of the car slammed on her brakes and banged on the horn at the same time. The car swerved, stopping just inches short of a parked jeep.

"Are you crazy?" The driver leaned out of the window and glared at Toby. "You could have been killed!"

Toby stared at her, white and shaking. "I-I'm sorry," she stammered. "I was—I was—"

"Our friend was very upset about something," Nancy said. "She didn't see you."

Bess put an arm around Toby's shoulder.

"Well, get her home before she hurts herself," the driver said crossly. She rolled up her window and drove away.

Nancy turned to look back toward the theater.

But the tall, gray-haired man who had recognized Toby had vanished.

Nancy was sipping a glass of orange juice the next morning when Bess sleepily opened one eye. Sunlight streamed through the windows of the main room. "Nan?" Bess mumbled.

"Yes, sleeping beauty?"

Bess sat up and stretched. "You're up already?"

"Up, showered, and dressed—after a morning swim, of course," Nancy replied.

Bess groaned. "This is a vacation, Nancy. Not scout camp. Remember?"

Nancy put down her glass and picked up her purse. "Lots of things to investigate today."

The door of the back bedroom opened, and Toby stepped out.

"Good morning," Nancy said. "Feeling better?"

"Much better." Toby blushed. "But I'm so embarrassed about last night. When I saw that man, I just had to get away."

"He scared you?" asked Bess.

"Either that, or—" Toby's voice rose in

frustration. "I don't know! I don't even know who he was!"

"That's what I'm going to find out," Nancy announced. "I took down the number of his car's license plate. I'm on my way into town to check it out. I'll give you guys a call if I learn anything interesting."

Before she stepped outside, Nancy added, "Toby, see if you can get Madame Suntan into the lake for a morning swim. The water's great!"

Half an hour later, Nancy approached the information counter of Minosha's police station. She put on a worried expression.

"Excuse me." She spoke timidly to the police sergeant behind the counter. "I wonder if you could possibly tell me who owns this car?" Nancy handed him the slip of paper on which she'd written the sedan's license number. "I think I may have sideswiped it," she added with a rueful smile.

The officer frowned. Obviously, he believed her. He took the slip over to a computer console. After a couple of minutes he came back to the counter. "I've got bad news," he told Nancy, shaking his head. "You hit the mayor's car."

"That blue sedan?" Nancy frowned in confusion. Why was Toby so afraid of the mayor?

33

The officer nodded sternly. "You're lucky you weren't arrested," he told her, then he smiled. "Look, this is a small town," he said. "We're all pretty casual. Just go to the mayor's office in Town Hall and talk with him face-to-face. His name is Ed Castle."

Nancy nodded. "I'll do that," she said. She reached into her purse for her car keys. Her fingers touched cold metal.

"Could I ask you one more thing?" She took the green WEB button out of her purse. "Do you know what this button stands for?"

The officer shook his head. He called back over his shoulder. "Sue! Do you know what WEB is?"

A woman officer came up to the counter. She examined the button Nancy showed her. "No. Sorry," she said.

"Well, thanks for your help," Nancy told them both.

Town Hall stood on High Street, Minosha's main thoroughfare. The street was lined with quaint, old wooden buildings standing right next to the sidewalk. It must have looked the same when Minosha was a tiny fishing village nearly a hundred years earlier.

A cozy-looking bookstore stood next to an ice-cream store where passersby could watch the ice cream being made in the window.

Facing the stores was a tiny park lined with benches.

Tourists in shorts and sandals wandered along the sidewalks, peering in the shop windows for souvenirs to buy.

At the end of the street, Nancy could see the large lake, a boat marina, and a ferry stop.

Nancy was tempted to explore the town. But there was no time for sight-seeing now. She hurried up the steps to Town Hall, a two-story building on the corner. A guard inside the lobby told her where to find the mayor's office on the second floor.

The door to the mayor's outer office was open, so Nancy walked in. "Good morning," she said to the woman sitting at the nearest desk. "I'm looking for someone named Toby Jackson. Do you know where I can find her?"

The woman looked startled. "Toby used to work here, but I'm afraid she was . . . well, fired recently. I don't know where she is."

A door at the end of the office opened, and the tall, gray-haired driver of the blue sedan stepped out.

"Mayor Castle," the woman at the desk called. "This young lady was asking about Toby Jackson."

"Toby?" The mayor turned his gaze on Nancy. "You know where she is?"

"No, sir," Nancy said as innocently as she could. "I'm trying to get in touch with her."

Mayor Castle stared at her. He seemed to be trying to decide whether Nancy was telling the truth. Nancy wondered if he recognized her from the night before.

"Toby no longer works here," Mayor Castle said at last. "She's in a great deal of trouble, too. Are you a friend of hers?"

"A friend of a friend," Nancy said. "I'm supposed to look her up."

"If you find her, please tell me right away," the mayor said. His forehead creased with concern. "I need to get in touch with her immediately."

"What happened?" Nancy asked.

The mayor sighed. "Toby stole important city documents," he explained. "It's a very serious offense. But Toby's young and inexperienced. We don't want to come down on her too hard. We just want her to give the documents back. If she does, we won't involve the police."

The mayor gave Nancy another searching look, as if he were wondering whether she knew more than she was saying.

"Are you from around here?" he asked. "I don't think I've seen you before."

"I'm just visiting for a few days," Nancy said.

"I see. Where are you staying?"

"In a cabin in the woods. It's very pretty." Nancy changed the subject. "This part of the state is lovely, Mayor Castle. I can see why your town's such a popular vacation spot."

The mayor didn't look pleased. "Beauty isn't everything," he murmured, as though to himself.

Nancy was surprised.

"I'd like to see more business in this town," the mayor said. "Minosha's crying out for more business. Business and industry are the way a town puts itself on the map. Not by sitting around staring at a lake with a bunch of tourists."

Nancy started to object, but the mayor broke in abruptly.

"Speaking of business, I've got to get some of my own done," he said. "Let me know right away if you hear anything from Toby Jackson." He shook her hand and turned back toward his office.

"I'll do my best, sir," Nancy answered. "Thanks very much for your help."

Nancy's mind was racing. Toby might really be a thief. Her amnesia could be just an act. What kind of important documents could she have stolen, and why?

37

It was time for some answers.

Nancy stepped onto High Street and started toward her car. A woman hurrying along the sidewalk ran smack into her, and Nancy's purse went flying.

"Excuse me!" the woman cried.

She picked up Nancy's purse and handed it to her, then hurried off.

Nancy caught a glimpse of the woman's collar. There was a green WEB button pinned to it.

"Wait!" Nancy ran after the woman. She swerved around a couple pushing their bikes. "I have to ask you something!"

The woman was almost at the end of the street. Nancy lost time in dodging a group of kids wearing huge backpacks, who were coming from the ferry station. When she had cleared the crowd of kids, Nancy saw the woman boarding the ferry. Nancy ran faster.

Nancy was only a few yards from the ferry dock. A foghorn blasted twice and the ferry conductor called, "All aboard!"

"Wait," she shouted. "I'm coming!"

Nancy reached the station platform, but the ferry conductor had grabbed the rope that tied the ferry to the dock. He swung the rope onto the deck at his feet.

The foghorn blasted again. The ferry was pulling away.

There was already a band of water between the platform and the ferry. Nancy gathered up all her strength and hurled herself across the dark water.

5

WEB of Intrigue

Nancy hit the edge of the ferryboat and stumbled backward. She waved her arms, trying to regain her balance.

"Help her!" a woman cried.

Like lightning, the ferry conductor stretched out his arm. He grabbed Nancy's wrist and yanked her onto the deck.

"What do you think you're doing?" the conductor shouted. "This isn't a circus, you know! You trying to fly or something?"

Nancy tried to catch her breath. The passengers all stared at her. She ignored them.

"I'm sorry," she gasped at last. "I wasn't thinking. I won't do it again."

"You'd better not," the conductor said. "Took ten years off my life. Crazy kids! . . . And what about your ticket? It costs a quarter to ride this ferry, you know."

Nancy took a quarter from her purse and handed it to the conductor. She made her way toward the back of the boat.

The woman with the WEB button was nowhere in sight. The ferry wasn't very big, so the woman had to be on it. At last Nancy spotted her in the covered section of the deck. She was sitting on the very last bench reading a magazine.

Nancy approached the woman. "Excuse me," she said. "May I ask you something?"

The woman had a sunny smile. "Sure," she said in a friendly voice.

"Would you tell me what that button means?" Nancy pointed to the small green disk. "I saw someone else wearing one, too."

"WEB?" The woman touched the button. "It stands for Wisconsin Ecological Balance. We're a group of people who are trying to save Wisconsin's land and water from being destroyed."

"What kind of people belong to WEB?" Nancy asked.

"All kinds," the woman replied. "We have lots of college students, some younger kids, and

41

older men and women, too. Would you like to join? We have a large membership here in Minosha."

"Here?" Nancy was surprised. "This area looks perfect."

"Yes, but we're worried about the future. Right now, Minosha has one of the cleanest lakes in the state. But there are people who hope to make money by building more factories and houses here. If they get their way, the lake will die."

"What do you mean?" Nancy asked.

"The lake could become polluted," the woman explained. "That will kill the fish and all the small animals and birds that need the lake for food."

She pointed to the shore of a nearby island. "Like those mallard ducks over there."

Nancy looked at the birds. They were lovely, with patterned wings and dark green heads.

"If the lake gets that bad, swimming will have to be banned," the woman said. "So there go all the tourists. Minosha would be a ghost town in no time."

Before Nancy could answer, the conductor shouted, "Little Isle! First stop—Little Isle!"

"I'm getting off here," Nancy said. She waved to the woman. "Thanks for the information."

"Think about becoming a member," the woman called after her.

Nancy got off the ferry and waited on the station platform for the next boat to Minosha.

Back at the Minosha station, she remembered the telephone message that had been in Toby's pocket. It had been signed "Sandy." Sandy was probably someone Toby had worked with at Town Hall.

Nancy decided to go back to Town Hall before heading back to the cabin. She needed as much information as she could get before she talked to Toby again.

She pushed through the heavy door to Town Hall for the second time that day.

"Back so soon?" the guard teased.

"Can't keep away." Nancy smiled at him. "I need to find someone named Sandy who works here," she explained. "But I don't know Sandy's last name."

"Might be more than one Sandy," the guard said. He pulled out the Town Hall directory. "But at least you're not looking for a John or a Mary." He ran his finger up and down the columns of employee names and office numbers.

"Here's a Sandy Barker," he said at last. "Works in the development department. Room two-thirty-four."

Nancy wrote it down as the guard read through more names.

"And Sandy Dorfman," the guard went on. "Works in the legal department, room two-thirty. And Sandy Lauffer. Records department. Room one-twelve. That's it for Sandys."

"Thanks a lot." Nancy headed for the stairs.

She found room 234 right away.

"Could I speak with Sandy Barker?" she asked the man sitting at the first desk.

He pointed to an inner office. "Right through that door." Nancy walked inside.

A woman was drawing at a high, slanted drafting table.

"Are you Sandy Barker?" Nancy asked.

The woman nodded without lifting her eyes. Her work looked complicated. She was drawing a three-story building that was new and modern looking.

"My name is Nancy Drew. I'm trying to get in touch with a Toby Jackson who worked here at Town Hall. Do you know her?"

"Toby Jackson?" Sandy Barker raised her blond head and thought for a minute. "No, I've never heard of her."

Nancy glanced down at the drawing. "Looks pretty fancy," she said.

"It's a blueprint—building plans," the

woman replied. "The mayor hopes a lot of new buildings will be going up around here."

The woman returned to her work. She was obviously very busy. Nancy glanced at her list of names and mentally crossed off Sandy Barker's.

"Thanks for your time," Nancy said. But the woman was working so hard she'd forgotten Nancy was there.

The next Sandy was in room 230. Sandy Dorfman turned out to be a slim young man. He had only been working at Town Hall for three weeks. He'd never heard of Toby, either.

Nancy walked down the stairs to room 112. The gold lettering on the door said Department of Records.

"Last Sandy, last chance," Nancy murmured as she opened the door.

A middle-aged woman with large blue-framed glasses and graying hair sat behind a counter.

"Sandy Lauffer?" Nancy asked.

"That's right," the woman replied.

Nancy introduced herself for the third time. "I'm trying to get in touch with the Toby Jackson who worked here. Do you know her, by any chance?"

Sandy Lauffer's eyes widened in surprise.

"Toby!" she said. "Is she a friend of yours? Do you know where she is?"

Nancy shook her head. "She's a friend of a friend. He asked me to check on Toby. He'd heard she was in trouble. Can you tell me what's going on? I really would like to help."

The woman started to speak, then closed her mouth. She glanced nervously at the door. "I-I'm not sure how much I can say," she murmured.

Nancy stepped closer. "Can you tell me what kind of work Toby did here?" she asked. "How long she'd been here? How long she's been gone?"

"She was a summer intern," Sandy said. "The mayor gives summer jobs to a couple of college students each year. It's a way of helping them get experience in local government."

"I think Toby was a student at the University of Wisconsin," Nancy said.

"That's right." Sandy nodded. "She was very bright."

"What did she do as an intern here?" Nancy asked.

Sandy looked uncomfortable. She answered in a low voice. "She was helping prepare a big report for the mayor's office."

"A report on what?"

46

This time Sandy shook her head. "I can't say. I don't want to make trouble."

Nancy paused. For a small tourist town, Minosha certainly had its share of mysteries. She decided to take a chance with Sandy Lauffer.

"I talked to Mayor Castle an hour or so ago," she said. "He told me that Toby stole some official documents. Is that the report you mean?"

Sandy looked very nervous.

"Oh, dear," she said. "I've never had to deal with anything like this before. I've been working in this building for twenty years, and I've always tried my best. I'm responsible for all the records."

"So the documents were taken from this department?" Nancy asked.

"Some of them." Sandy Lauffer looked close to tears. "All of us were very upset—and shocked, too. Toby seemed like such a nice girl. I can't believe she'd steal anything."

"Can you tell me anything else about her work here?" Nancy asked.

Sandy shook her head. "I don't even know if I should be talking to you at all. I'm so confused about this whole thing. For twenty years . . ."

"Maybe you can tell me this," Nancy said. "Where did Toby live in Minosha? If you can just tell me where, I might be able to find out something that can help everyone."

Sandy looked happy to change the subject.

"She was staying at a guest house on Gorham Street," Sandy told her. "The Gorham Inn."

"Thanks," Nancy said. "I really will try to help. And I'll let you know if I find out anything important."

Nancy had a lot on her mind. But it was a quarter to two. She was too hungry for more investigating. She stared down High Street, wondering whether there was anywhere besides the picturesque, expensive cafés to buy a lunch.

Finally she saw a sign reading Overstuffed Sandwiches in a deli window. Perfect, she said to herself. She walked in and went straight to the take-out counter.

"One tuna with lettuce and mayo on a hard roll, to go," she said to the counterman.

Nancy strolled back to the parking lot where she'd left the car. As she walked she glanced in the windows of the boutiques that lined the sidewalk.

There was Bess's white dress with the dropped waist. Nancy rolled her eyes when she saw the price tag. Bess was in for a big surprise.

Nancy reached her car and unlocked the door. The car was hot and stuffy after sitting for so long in the strong sun. She opened all the windows and sat with the driver's door open while she ate her sandwich.

Now to the Gorham Inn, Nancy said to herself when she'd finished eating. She closed the car door and turned on the ignition. She backed out of the parking space and headed out of the small lot.

Just as Nancy turned into the street, something hit the front of her car with tremendous force.

Crack!

A heavy object rolled off the car. It had left a small mark on the windshield.

Nancy slammed on the brakes. Another object flew into the windshield.

Someone was attacking her car!

6

A Threatening Note

For a split second Nancy froze. She scanned the parking lot. No one was nearby. Her heart pounding, she turned off the ignition and jumped out of the car.

Resting on the hood of the car was a fist-sized object wrapped in white paper. She was lucky it hadn't broken the windshield. Cautiously Nancy unwrapped the paper.

Inside was a large rock. Someone had scrawled a message on the piece of paper.

LEAVE TOBY ALONE!

Nancy glanced around the parking lot once more to make sure no one was hiding behind a parked car.

She tucked the piece of paper into her purse, climbed back into her own car, and locked all the doors before she began driving again.

She was shaken up. Everyone she'd talked to so far had wanted Nancy to *find* Toby. Yet someone wanted her to leave Toby unfound.

Did that someone also want Toby to have amnesia? Nancy didn't like that thought. They would all have to watch Toby more closely. They would all have to keep Toby safe. It was about time Nancy learned more about her new friend.

The Gorham Inn was at the end of a quiet block of big old houses. Lovely maples and oaks shaded the front lawn.

A stern-faced woman appeared at the front door as Nancy walked up the path. "May I help you?" she asked.

"I hope so," Nancy answered. "Are you Toby Jackson's landlady?"

"Yes. Mrs. Clerican's my name. Who are you?"

"Nancy Drew. I'm afraid Toby may be in some trouble. I was wondering if I could look through her room?"

51

Mrs. Clerican frowned. "I can't let just anyone into my guests' rooms," she said. "How would you like it if you were a guest?"

"I wouldn't like it. But I'm a friend of Toby's and I think she's in trouble," Nancy repeated. "I want to help her. Did you know she didn't come home last night?"

"Of course I know that," Mrs. Clerican snapped. Then she blushed. "That is, I don't check up on my guests, but . . ."

"No one knows where Toby is," Nancy bluffed. "There might be something in her room that could help me find her. Would you take me to Toby's room and stay there while I look around?"

Mrs. Clerican hesitated. "Well . . . you seem like a nice girl," she finally said. "And if Toby's in trouble, I want to help. I guess you can look around for a little while."

She led the way to a small second-floor bedroom.

"Not much to see," she commented. "She's a very neat girl. Not like some."

Nancy went through Toby's clothes and belongings. Several books on ecology were stacked on her desk. There were a few magazines on the bed.

"Did she have a purse?" Nancy asked. "Or an address book or a briefcase?"

Mrs. Clerican shrugged. "She must have them with her," she said.

"And you didn't see her leave?"

"No. I was with my sister all day. Her grandson's having his tenth birthday, and we . . ."

"That sounds like fun," Nancy cut in. She could see the woman wanted to chat, but Nancy didn't have time for that.

"Thank you, Mrs. Clerican. I appreciate your help."

Nancy pulled out of Gorham Street, lost in thought. Suddenly a small sign caught her eye. She slammed on the brakes and backed up several yards.

"The Boat Yard Café," Nancy said out loud, staring at the sign. It hung over a small, run-down coffee shop. Maybe this was the boat yard in Toby's note! Boat yard 2:30.

With a sense of excitement, Nancy walked into the coffee shop. A long counter lined with stools filled one wall. Several tables covered with red-checked plastic tablecloths were placed in the center of the room. A man sat in a booth near the door, drinking coffee and reading a newspaper. Another man stood behind the counter washing some glasses.

Nancy spoke to the man behind the counter.

53

"I'm looking for a young woman named Toby Jackson. Do you know her?"

"Doesn't ring a bell," the man said. "But ask him. Mr. Wood. He meets a lot of folks here."

The man pointed to the table by the door. "Hey, Donald! This lady's looking for someone named Toby."

Wood! Nancy's pulse raced. Boat yard. Wood. At last, she was getting somewhere.

Donald Wood was a handsome man, about twenty-five years old, with dark hair and eyes. He wore faded jeans and a light blue work shirt. There was a long scratch running along the left side of his face. Nancy shivered. She thought of the blood under Toby's fingernails.

Wood spoke before Nancy could say anything. "What do you know about Toby Jackson?" His dark eyes were not friendly.

"I'm a friend of a friend," Nancy said. "I've been trying to get in touch with Toby."

"How did you end up here?" Wood demanded.

Nancy was surprised at the man's angry tone. She decided not to answer him.

"Have you seen Toby lately?" she asked him.

Wood leaned back and shook his head.

"When was the last time you *did* see Toby?"

He looked even more angry. "Why should I tell you anything?" he demanded.

"I know you were supposed to meet Toby here," Nancy went on.

Wood frowned. "How did you know that?" He rose from his seat. "You must have talked to her yourself."

Nancy stepped back. Wood looked dangerous.

"If you won't speak to me, I guess I won't take up any more of your time. Thanks, anyway, Mr. Wood."

Nancy quickly left the café.

"Why didn't you ask him more questions?" George asked.

Nancy had returned to the cabin and told the other girls about her meeting with Wood.

"I could see he wasn't going to tell me anything," Nancy explained. "And I didn't want to give him any idea of where Toby was. I thought it would be safest to cut the conversation short."

Nancy frowned. "We need to know if Toby trusts Wood. I have a feeling Toby did meet him—with some pretty terrible results."

Nancy had headed straight home from the Boat Yard Café. Bess and George had been waiting eagerly for her. She filled them in on the trips to Town Hall, the ride on the ferry, and the message thrown at her car. But she hadn't told Toby about the stolen documents.

Toby sat curled up under a blanket on one of the beds in the back room. She looked tired and frail.

"Toby," Nancy said, "I talked to Mayor Castle today. He had some news about you."

She looked the girl in the eye. "I'm afraid it wasn't good news. Would you like me to tell you about it in private?"

"You mean without Bess and George?" Toby looked at the other girls. "No, that's okay. You've all been so nice to me—I don't mind if they hear whatever it is."

"All right, then." Nancy took a deep breath. "He said you stole important papers. Official documents."

Toby's face turned white. "I—I can hardly believe that! I could go to jail for that, couldn't I?"

Nancy nodded. "I'm afraid so. I also met someone you might know." Nancy paused. "Donald Wood. I met him at the Boat Yard Café. To be honest, I don't know if he's your friend or your enemy."

Toby looked ill. "I don't know, either," she whispered. "I can't remember."

"What documents could Minosha have that

anyone would want to steal?" George sprang to Toby's defense. "I don't believe any of it."

"I don't, either," Bess said. "Toby doesn't seem like a criminal to me." Bess crossed her arms. She looked angry.

Nancy felt awful. "I'm afraid I *do* believe it," she said.

Toby cried out. "No! I'm not a thief. There must be some reason, some explanation."

"I think so, too." Nancy sat on the edge of the bed. She grasped Toby's hand.

"Try—try to remember."

Toby squeezed her eyes shut. "Wood," she murmured. "Donald Wood . . ." She shook her head. "Nothing. It's all a blank."

"Try harder," Nancy told her.

An expression of horror flashed across Toby's face. "Wait," she whispered. "I—I just saw a brown leather briefcase—and I was putting some typed pages into it. Oh, Nancy!" Her voice trembled. "It is true, I *did* steal the papers. Are you going to call the police?"

Nancy shook her head. "Not yet. Not until we know the reason why."

Nancy was taking a risk, and she knew it. The courts should decide if Toby had a good reason to take the papers. But Toby's forty-eight hours weren't over yet. Toby deserved a chance to prove she was innocent.

"I just remembered something else," Toby said. "I was running. To give something—the papers, I think—to someone. And a man was chasing me."

"Can you remember anything about him?" Nancy asked.

Toby closed her eyes for a moment. "Maybe he was wearing a blue shirt," she answered.

"Hmmm," Nancy said. "Not much help."

"Listen," George interrupted. "Someone's coming down the path!"

Footsteps sounded outside. They grew louder and louder. Someone stepped heavily onto the front porch.

There was a sharp rapping at the door. Toby jumped to her feet.

"Just a minute," Nancy called in a casual voice. She motioned to Toby to stay quiet and shut the bedroom door.

George ran lightly to the front window and peeked through the curtains.

"It's the police!"

7

Toby Disappears . . . Again!

Nancy smoothed her hair and walked calmly to the front door.

A young man in a dark blue police uniform took off his hat and smiled at her. He had wavy, light brown hair and blue eyes. Nancy couldn't help but notice how handsome he was.

"Hello," he said. "My name's Richard Banner. I'm one of Mayor Castle's assistants. May I talk to you for a minute?"

"Okay." Nancy stepped out onto the porch. She placed herself between the man and the cabin door. "You're a police officer?" she asked.

"Not really. I'm a member of the auxiliary

police. It's a volunteer organization. We help out with routine police chores, like school crossings and parade duty. Nothing very exciting, I'm afraid. I've just come from a meeting —that's why I'm dressed like this."

He smiled again. "Usually I look like an ordinary guy."

Nancy smiled, too. She was glad the police weren't on Toby's trail.

"I was in the mayor's office when you stopped by this morning," Banner said. "I heard you say you were looking for Toby Jackson. If you find her, let her know that no one wants to make trouble for her. I knew her some, and she's a really nice kid."

"Can you tell me what happened?" Nancy asked.

Banner shrugged. "I don't know what kind of documents she took. Or what kind of report she was working on. To be frank, it's none of my business. I'm in charge of the mayor's staff— not his reports. I learned a long time ago— don't get involved if you don't have to."

"So what are you doing out here?" Nancy put on a little smile.

"I like Toby." Banner looked embarrassed. "I thought this whole thing could be straightened out if she returned the documents. The mayor is a pretty nice guy."

He paused. "You haven't found out where Toby is, have you?"

"No," Nancy replied. "But if I do, I'll let her know what you said."

Richard Banner stood on tiptoe and looked over her shoulder into the cabin.

"Could we finish talking inside?" he suggested. "It's a little cold out here."

Nancy thought quickly.

"I wish we could, but my friend Bess is sleeping. A bad case of sun poisoning. She stayed out too long on our first day here."

Banner grinned. "I know what that's like, believe me. I burn the second I get outside. Anyway, if you need me for anything, here's my phone number at work." He took a pen and paper out of his pocket and wrote down his number.

"By the way," Nancy asked, "how did you know where I was staying? I don't think I mentioned this place in the mayor's office."

Banner grinned again. "You said you were staying in a cabin in the woods," he said. "I made a few calls. It was easy to find out who was renting to a pretty strawberry blond."

Nancy almost blushed. "I see." She took the slip of paper he held out.

"Please, call me," he repeated as he put his cap back on.

He waved as he started up the path.

Nancy stepped back into the cabin.

Bess waited until Banner could no longer hear them. "What do you think?"

"We were listening at the window," George added. "He seems like a nice guy."

"Cute, too," Bess added.

"He seemed nice," Nancy said slowly. "But I don't understand why he's so interested in Toby. Why did he come all the way out here if he doesn't want to be involved?"

"Maybe he's secretly in love with her," Bess suggested.

Nancy frowned. "Then why would he hide it?" She shrugged. "Banner may be okay. But I'm not making up my mind one way or the other—yet."

"Let's give Toby the all clear," George said. "She looked as if she were going to faint when I said the police were here."

George tapped on the bedroom door before opening it. She peeked inside, and gasped.

"Toby's gone!" she cried.

Nancy and Bess raced into the bedroom.

A breeze was blowing the curtains into the room. The screen had been removed, and the window was wide open.

Nancy looked grim. "Come on. We've got to find her."

62

The three girls ran out the front door. There was no sign of Toby.

They circled around to the back of the cabin, where the path led down to the dock.

"She might be in the woods somewhere. Let's split up and start looking."

"No way," Bess objected. "I tried that yesterday, remember? With my luck, I'll run into the redheaded guy again."

Nancy shook her head. "I doubt you'll come across him a second time. He'll probably never go near the woods again after hearing you scream! But it's fine with me if we search together."

The girls edged into the woods between the dock and the cabin. Only a dim light filtered through the trees. The late afternoon sun was low in the sky. The woods were silent except for the crackling of leaves and branches underfoot.

"Ouch!" George yelped. She stopped to examine her ankle. "These darn branches. I'm getting cut to pieces."

"Ditto," Bess said. "I wouldn't mind a paved path to walk on—or a sidewalk. Don't you guys think it's pretty creepy in here?"

"Come on, Bess," Nancy urged. "I know it's hard, but don't give up on us. Think how scared Toby must feel."

She plunged forward into the underbrush. George and Bess followed close behind.

"She must be close by," Bess said.

"Toby!" Nancy called. "It's okay to come out now. There's nothing to be afraid of!"

Her only answer was the leaves rustling around her.

Nancy took a few more steps and tripped over a tree root. She fell to her knees.

She reached out a hand to push herself back up and felt something soft and warm.

It didn't move. At first she thought it was an animal, perhaps injured.

Nancy peered closer and gasped. It wasn't an animal at all.

It was Toby.

8

Someone Looking In

"What is it, Nan?" Bess and George were beside her.

"Toby's been hurt." Nancy knelt beside the girl's body and gently tried to turn her over. George and Bess watched.

Toby stirred and gave a faint moan.

"She's okay!" Nancy cried. She brushed some dry leaves from Toby's face.

"Toby?" she asked gently. "Are you all right?"

Toby's eyes opened, but she looked completely dazed.

"Can you talk?" Nancy asked.

Toby nodded. "I'm okay," she said.

"Take it easy," Nancy cautioned. "George—Bess—give me a hand."

With the help of all three girls, Toby was able to sit up. She breathed deeply a few times.

"I think I got the wind knocked out of me," she explained after a second. "I'm sorry. I must have scared you to death."

"Well, as a matter of fact . . ." Bess murmured. Even in the dark Nancy could see that Bess was pale.

"I panicked. It was that police officer," Toby explained. "I know it's stupid, but I thought he was going to arrest me. And there was something else, too—a feeling I don't understand. As if he were out to hurt me." She drew in a long, shaky breath.

"He wasn't a real police officer," Nancy said. She explained who Richard Banner was and why he'd come. "What happened after you left the cabin?" she asked.

"I just started running," Toby said. "I wasn't watching where I was going—I just had to get away. I tripped over something and fell."

Nancy nodded. "It's safe in the cabin now." She stood up. "We should get you back there," she said. "It's pretty damp out here."

The girls helped Toby back to the cabin.

Nancy didn't say so, but she was glad Toby

66

had tripped. At least they knew no one had pushed her. They still had no idea who Toby's enemy was.

"Does that name—Richard Banner—sound familiar?" Nancy asked.

Toby shook her head. "When I try to think of names," she said, "the same one comes to me, over and over. 'Castle.' That's all—just 'Castle.' Maybe it's because you told me about meeting the mayor today. But it seems like it's more than that."

Nancy and George piled pillows on one of the sofa beds so Toby could relax.

Bess searched through the kitchen cabinets. "Where are the rest of those taco chips?" she asked. "I'm starving."

"How about a sunset swim instead?" George suggested. "Then we'll really deserve a good dinner."

"Frankly, I think we deserve one anyway," Bess replied. "But a swim sounds great. How about you, Nan?"

Nancy looked at Toby. "Will you be all right by yourself for a little while? You can lock the cabin door."

"I'll be fine," Toby said. "Don't worry about me. I'm too comfortable here to move." She added with a little laugh, "And I promise I'll be here when you get back."

Nancy, Bess, and George changed quickly into their bathing suits and jogged down to the dock.

"Last one in gets no dessert!" George dove neatly into the water. Nancy and Bess were right behind her.

The smooth surface of the water reflected the pinks and corals of the sunset sky. The trees cast dark shadows around the edges of the lake.

Nancy did a slow breaststroke, keeping her head above water so she could enjoy the view.

"This is heaven." She sighed when Bess and George paddled up to her.

"We should try a late-night swim, too," George suggested. "That's really fun."

"Not tonight," said Nancy. "At least not for me. I have a few things to check out."

"Like what?" Bess wanted to know.

"First I'm going back to the theater," Nancy answered. "The Castle Community Theater. I still think it might be why the name Castle seems so important to Toby."

"That's a good idea," Bess said. "Remember last night, how frightened Toby was when she saw the theater sign?"

Nancy turned and floated on her back.

"I think I'll poke around town a little, too. And maybe go back to the Boat Yard Café. I want to find out more about that Donald Wood."

"I'll go with you this time," George offered.

"Great," Nancy said. "I could use some help. You know, Toby's forty-eight hours run out tomorrow afternoon. I don't know about you two—but I'm beginning to worry about not getting Toby to a doctor."

The girls climbed onto the dock and dried themselves with their towels.

"I'm worried, too," Bess confessed. "Not only about Toby's health, but about—well, whether she's done something really criminal. I mean, I don't believe she did—but not being sure is kind of a strain. Do you really think we'll find out what this whole thing is about by tomorrow afternoon, though?"

"I don't know," Nancy answered as she dried her hair. "If I can find out what report Toby was working on and what documents are gone, we might be a lot further along."

Back in the cabin, the three girls found that Toby had already set the table.

"I started broiling the chicken," she said, "but I wasn't sure what you had planned to go with it."

"Garlic bread and salad," Bess said promptly. "Do you think we need something else? Potatoes? String beans?"

69

"Nothing more," said Nancy. "We have mint chocolate-chip ice cream for dessert. Remember?"

"Okay," Bess said. "I'll see how the chicken is doing."

"Toby, are you too tired to answer one more question before we eat?" asked Nancy.

Toby did look tired but she shook her head. "Ask away," she said.

"Let's suppose you're a member of WEB," Nancy began. "If you are, you must know something about ecology and the environment. What can you remember about the kinds of things that could hurt a lake like Lake Minosha?"

Toby thought a moment. "Well, factories are one thing. They produce a lot of waste. Unless they're carefully controlled, they can badly pollute the water. Another thing is too many people living on the lake."

"Why?" Nancy asked.

"The ecology of a place is a delicate balance of a lot of different lives," Toby explained. "If you throw off the balance, the whole system falls apart. Too many people mean too many motorboats—motorboats are big polluters. And when you build lots of houses by a lake, that means fewer water birds and other lake creatures can live there."

"The chicken's almost ready," Bess said. "Can we continue this discussion while we eat?"

"Sure," Toby said. "But can I get an aspirin first? I still have a headache."

"I'll get you one," said Nancy.

"Good luck," Bess said. "That medicine cabinet is a mess."

Bess was right. They had only been in the cabin for one day, and already the medicine cabinet was crammed full of shampoos, hairbrushes, lotions, creams, nail files, foot powders, and tubes of toothpaste.

"Like finding a needle in a haystack," Nancy muttered.

She heard a soft rustling outside. She glanced at the open bathroom window, but saw nothing unusual out there.

Nancy thought it must be some kind of wild animal. She spotted the aspirin bottle behind a bottle of mouthwash.

As she reached for it, she heard another noise. Much closer this time.

Nancy whirled. On the other side of the window was a face—the face of a man watching her.

9

Yellow Convertible

Nancy screamed, and the man at the window turned and ran.

Nancy raced out of the bathroom and almost collided with George, who had come running in at the sound of her scream.

"A man was at the window, spying on me," Nancy panted. "We've got to catch him!"

She and George raced out the front door.

"I think he went that way." Nancy pointed toward the office.

In the beam from the light hanging over the office door, they could see a redheaded man racing down the path. Nancy and George dashed after him.

They'd reached the clearing in front of the office when they heard the roar of a car engine.

"Look!" George pointed toward the dirt drive that led to the main road.

A car rounded the curve. It was the yellow convertible.

"We lost him again," Nancy cried. She and George stared after the car. Then they turned and walked back to the cabin.

Bess and Toby were waiting with frightened faces.

"Did you see who it was?" Bess asked.

"You're not going to believe this," Nancy said. "It was the guy in the yellow convertible again. We saw him drive away."

Bess shivered. "I don't like this, Nancy. What's he doing around here, spying on us like this?"

Before Nancy could answer, Toby spoke up. "He must be spying on me. Maybe he's tracking me down."

"I hate to agree with you," Nancy said. "But I think you must be right. I'm going to call the office right now to let Mr. Wickman know what happened. I'll ask him to keep an eye out for strangers or unknown cars."

Once Nancy had made the call, the girls sat down to dinner. But no one had much of an appetite—not even Bess.

After dinner, Nancy and George got ready to go into Minosha.

"Better bring a flashlight, George," said Nancy. "It's awfully dark out there."

"We'll do the dishes for you," Bess offered.

"Thanks," said Nancy. "Are you guys sure you'll be okay alone?"

"Sure," said Bess stoutly. "We can play cards or something. We'll have a great time."

George turned on her flashlight as she and Nancy walked across the porch.

"Nancy, you must have dropped this." George bent down to pick up a small round object. She handed it to Nancy.

Puzzled, Nancy opened her purse and pulled out an identical button.

"This is the one Toby gave me," she said. "Maybe that other one belongs to Richard Banner. He was standing on the porch."

She slipped both buttons into her purse. She would hunt down the owner later.

Nancy and George drove toward town. As they passed the tarred part of the road, George sat up.

"I just thought of something," she said. "The red-haired guy in the yellow convertible might be a friend of Toby's. Maybe he's trying to find her. And that's why he said, 'Where is she?' to Bess."

"Could be," Nancy said slowly. "That could be why he was sneaking around our cabin. But why does he keep running away? Toby's terrified of something—and it might be him."

Nancy pulled into the parking lot of the Castle Community Theater.

"It's crowded again," George said, looking at the rows and rows of parked cars.

"I guess the production is pretty good," Nancy said. "Maybe we should get tickets— once this mystery is solved."

She glanced at her watch. "It's eight-forty-five. The play's already started. Maybe we can find an usher who will talk to us."

The girls walked into the theater lobby. It was empty, except for a young woman in an usher's uniform. She was sitting on a stool, reading a book.

"Excuse me," Nancy said. The young woman looked up.

"I was just wondering how this theater got its name. Did the Castle family build it?"

The usher nodded. "They sure did. And the hospital. And the library. And they probably own most of High Street. The Castles are the richest family in Minosha."

"How did they make all that money?" Nancy asked. "Is there a family business?"

"Lumber," the usher answered. "They've

75

been in the business for about a hundred years. I think the great-grandfather started the company."

"And the mayor is from the same family?" Nancy asked.

"Of course! He doesn't work for the family while he's mayor, though. His brother owns the company. All the Castles are like royalty in Minosha. Why do you want to know all this, anyway?"

"I'm from out of town," Nancy explained. "I was just curious about the name. Thanks for your help."

She and George walked back to the car before the usher could ask any more questions. As they pulled out of the parking lot, George asked, "Do you think Toby remembers the name Castle because the family is famous or because she worked for the mayor?"

Nancy shook her head. "There's no way of knowing. But Toby was really frightened by the Castle Theater sign last night. Whichever Castle she's trying to remember must be pretty dangerous. The mayor didn't look scary at all. Maybe it's someone else in the family."

Nancy drove into the center of Minosha. High Street was so crowded with tourists that Nancy had trouble finding a parking space. Japanese lanterns lit the sidewalks, and outdoor cafés were adorned with strings of tiny white lights.

"All these people," George said. "It's like a parade up and down the sidewalk."

Nancy smiled. "The tourists here must spend half their vacations looking at each other."

Finally they found a spot for the car on a side street. Then they made their way to the ferry station.

From the dock, Nancy and George watched the ferry lights shimmer on the water. In the distance, they could make out the lights in the houses on nearby Little Isle.

"The town's really pretty, isn't it?" George commented.

Nancy agreed.

"Nan, why don't we do some people-watching ourselves?" George suggested. "I wouldn't mind having a soda at one of the cafés."

Nancy looked back toward High Street.

"How about that one?" She pointed to a café with a second-floor terrace. "I'll bet you can see everything from up there."

"Looks great to me," George said.

They found seats toward the front of the terrace and ordered sodas. They settled back to watch the crowd.

"Very relaxing," Nancy remarked. "Wasn't that what this vacation was supposed to be?" she asked. "Relaxing?"

"Right, Nan," George said with a laugh. "You're a real pro at that."

"I'll bet I'll relax more after I've . . ."

Someone tapped Nancy on the shoulder. She turned around. It was Richard Banner, the mayor's assistant.

"Hi, Nancy," he said. "Enjoying the local nightlife?"

Nancy smiled. "We were just saying how much fun it is to sit and watch."

"Mind if I join you for a minute?" he asked.

"That would be nice," Nancy said. "This is my friend George Fayne. She's staying at the cabin with me. George, this is Richard Banner."

He smiled at George. "Are you the one with the sun poisoning? You seem to have recovered awfully fast."

"No, that's our other friend," Nancy said quickly. "I was telling Mr. Banner all about poor Bess's attack of the sun rays, George. She was feeling too horrible for him to come in, wasn't she?"

She stepped lightly on George's foot as she spoke.

Fortunately, George caught on immediately.

"Yes, Bess really overdid it," she said. "I think she'll be okay tomorrow, though."

Banner sat down. "Please call me Richard. Any news about Toby?"

Nancy pressed George's foot again. "Not a thing. How about you?"

Banner shook his head. "Do you know Toby?" he asked George.

"No," George said. "But I heard about her from Nancy." She smiled. "I guess you'd say I'm a friend of a friend of a friend."

Nancy glanced toward the busy street. Suddenly her eyes widened. She leaned forward.

"Don't look," she said to George in a low voice, "but there's the guy with the curly red hair, in front of the shoe store." She nodded his way.

George jumped to her feet. "That's him," she shouted. "The Peeping Tom—don't let him get away!"

10

Stolen Documents

At the sound of George's voice, the red-haired man spun around. His eyes met Richard Banner's. He started to run.

"Get him!" George shouted.

George dashed after him. Nancy hesitated. "Do you know him?" she asked Banner.

"He's a stranger to me," Banner said simply. Nancy believed him.

"Lost him," George said when Nancy and Banner caught up to her.

"What's this about a Peeping Tom?" Banner asked. Nancy nodded at George to tell her it was okay. George blushed. She realized she shouldn't have shouted in front of Banner without knowing if Banner and the redhead were working together.

"We caught him spying in our cabin window," Nancy explained. "We chased him, but he got away. Now he's escaped again."

Banner frowned. "Don't worry," he assured them. "If he's from around here, I'm sure I'll run into him again. And I won't let him get away next time. This is a nice, quiet town. We don't put up with Peeping Toms."

An angry voice called from the café terrace. "Hey, you girls! You didn't pay for your drinks." A frowning waiter stared down at them.

"We're coming right back," George called up.

"We'd better get up there before they call the police," Nancy said with a chuckle.

The girls said goodbye to Banner and climbed the terrace steps to pay their bill. A few minutes later they were on their way back to the car.

Just as they reached the car, Nancy stopped and slapped her forehead. "Guess what I forgot?" she said. "I didn't ask Banner about the WEB button."

George shrugged. "Oh, well. You can find him tomorrow."

Nancy agreed. "Let's head over to the Boat

Yard Café," she said. "If that's okay with you, I mean."

"Why not?" George replied. "Café-hopping is very trendy these days, right?"

The girls got into the car, and Nancy started the engine. "Trendy is not the word I'd use to describe the Boat Yard," she said. "Seedy, yes. Trendy, no. So prepare yourself."

When they stepped into the café, George whistled softly. "You weren't kidding, were you?"

Nancy glanced around the dingy coffee shop. Donald Wood wasn't there. Almost all the booths were empty. The only waitress in sight stood hunched over the counter, flipping the pages of a magazine.

Nancy walked up to her.

"Hi," she said. "I wonder if you can help me. I'm looking for a Mr. Wood. I think he comes in here sometimes."

"Oh, sure," the waitress answered. "I know who you mean. He wasn't here tonight, though."

"Do you know where I could find him?"

"Well—he's staying at the Castle Avenue Hotel," the woman answered.

Nancy and George eyed each other. Another Castle!

"Are you a friend of his?" the waitress asked. "There are always people coming in here looking for him."

"Not really," Nancy said. "But I'm supposed to get in touch with him. I guess he's not from Minosha if he's staying in a hotel."

"No, he's not from around here," the waitress said. "But he's been hanging out for a few weeks. Drinks a lot of coffee and reads a lot of newspapers."

"Where's his hotel exactly?" Nancy asked.

"Near the corner of Vauxhall and Castle," the waitress replied. "You can't miss it. It has one of those old neon signs outside."

Nancy and George thanked the waitress and went back to the car.

"This Wood character sounds suspicious," George declared. "He's from out of town—he meets lots of people in that seedy café—and he might have had a meeting with Toby. And there's a scratch on his face. I think Toby put it there. Plus, we find out that he's staying at the Castle Avenue Hotel! That's why Toby's afraid of the word *Castle*."

"Sounds convincing." Nancy grinned. "But we don't know what really happened. Did Toby steal the documents to give them to Wood? Or did someone steal them from her?"

Nancy shook her head. "It would help if we knew what those documents were about. Then we'd know who really wanted them."

Nancy drove down High Street to Castle Avenue.

"I'd like to meet the Castles," she remarked. "They might know what's really going on."

"They can be next," George remarked. "After we talk to Wood."

"Let's play this by ear," Nancy said. They were nearing the hotel where the waitress had said Wood was staying. "It wasn't easy to get him to talk before."

Nancy parked across from the Castle Avenue Hotel.

"Look at this place," George said. "It's almost as seedy as the Boat Yard Café."

Two of the letters in the neon sign outside the hotel were broken. The paint was peeling, and the front porch sagged. As Nancy and George walked in, the screen door creaked. But though the furnishings were old-fashioned and shabby, the lobby was clean.

Nancy spotted the clerk dozing behind the reception desk. His chair was tipped back against the wall and a newspaper was draped over his face.

"Excuse me," Nancy said.

The clerk snorted, but went on sleeping.

Nancy saw a brass bell on the counter. She tapped it once, and it let out a loud clang. The sleeping clerk sat up with a start.

"What?" He looked very confused. Then he saw the two girls.

"Oh." He rubbed his eyes. "Must have dozed off. What can I do for you?"

"We'd like to see Mr. Wood," Nancy said. "He's in room eighteen."

Actually, Nancy had no idea which room Wood was staying in. Giving a number was an old detective's trick.

"No Mr. Wood in eighteen," the clerk said. "He's staying in room six."

"Oh, of course. Is that on this floor?" Nancy asked.

The clerk yawned and nodded. "Just down that corridor." He waved his hand to the left.

Nancy and George went in that direction.

"Hey, wait a minute!" the clerk said loudly.

Nancy stopped halfway down the hall.

"I'll call him for you," the clerk said.

"That's okay," Nancy called back. "We're friends of his."

The clerk shrugged, leaned back against the wall again, and closed his eyes.

"Nice work," George whispered to Nancy.

Room six was at the far end of the corridor. Nancy rapped on the door. There was no answer. She knocked again, louder this time. Still no answer.

"Let's find out when he'll be back," Nancy suggested.

The girls retraced their steps back to the lobby. As Nancy approached the reception desk, the clerk half opened his eyes.

"Not there?" he asked, yawning again. "Not surprised. He always stays out late. Usually doesn't get back until midnight."

"Maybe we'll be back then," Nancy announced loudly. "Come on, George. Let's go home."

As soon as they were out of the hotel, Nancy beckoned to George.

"Follow me," she whispered.

She ducked around the side of the hotel and began walking rapidly to the back.

"Stay in the shadows," she murmured to George.

"I didn't think we were giving up," George whispered.

"Absolutely not," Nancy whispered back. "It's time we learned some facts."

They were at the back of the hotel. It was easy to figure out that the middle window on the first floor belonged to room six. But the window was too high to reach.

"Help me move this trash can," Nancy said in a low voice.

George picked up one side of the heavy can.

"If Wood won't talk to us, we'll have to find another way to get the answers we need." Nancy took a deep breath. "Wood might have information that will help Toby get her memory back. We don't have a choice."

She scrambled up onto the trash can.

"My guess is that the locks in a place like this don't work very well."

George held the trash can steady, and Nancy pushed the window as hard as she could.

It opened easily.

"Should I come in with you?" George whispered.

"Stand guard—for now."

Nancy boosted herself up to the sill. She swung her legs over the ledge, then lowered herself inside.

She found the flashlight in her purse and switched it on. The rumpled bed was strewn with clothes. A huge stack of newspapers sat on one of the chairs. Nancy flipped through the papers. About half were copies of the *Minosha Daily News*. The other papers came from other Wisconsin towns and from Chicago.

Nancy trained her flashlight on the other

side of the room. A large map of the Minosha area lay on the floor. More newspapers and several notebooks covered the top of the desk. A portable typewriter and telephone sat to one side.

Nancy leafed through the papers. There was a large manila envelope addressed to Donald Wood. The return address read, "Arthur Ferranti, Department of Environmental Studies, University of Wisconsin, Madison."

The envelope was empty.

Under the envelope, Nancy found two clippings from the *Minosha Daily News.* One had been published three weeks earlier. Its headline read, New Castle Mill Will Not Pollute Lake.

The second clipping was just a week old. Its headline read, Castles' Plans for Paper Mill Approved.

"More Castles," Nancy murmured under her breath. She was just starting to read the first article when something caught her eye.

Half hidden under some papers was a thick stack of documents. Nancy's heart started beating hard. She pulled the papers out. Stamped across the top, in large red letters, was the word *Confidential.* Directly underneath were the words *Department of Records, Minosha City Government.*

88

The stolen documents!

Her heart was pounding. Quickly, Nancy opened the report to the first page.

Rapid footsteps sounded in the corridor. They were coming her way.

Nancy put the papers back.

A key turned in the door to the room. Nancy darted to the closet and slipped inside.

11

What's the Scoop?

With a faint creak, the room door swung open.

Heavy footsteps sounded in the room. Something was dropped onto the desk.

The footsteps came toward the closet.

Nancy pressed herself back into the corner behind some clothes. Her shoulders and head were hidden, but if Wood opened the door, he would be sure to see the rest of her.

The closet door opened. Nancy held her breath. An arm reached in and grabbed a hanger. The arm missed Nancy by inches.

A few seconds later, the arm reappeared. It hung a jacket on the clothes rod. The closet door shut.

Slowly, Nancy let out her breath.

The footsteps moved away again. Papers shuffled. Nancy heard a yawn. Wood walked toward the bathroom. A second later, Nancy heard him brushing his teeth.

If Wood takes a shower, I can sneak away, Nancy thought.

The water began to run. Nancy got ready to let herself out, but then the telephone rang.

Wood hurried out of the bathroom.

"Wood here," he said into the phone.

There was a pause as he listened.

"Tonight? Hey, it's late, and I'm beat. I was just getting in the shower."

There was another pause, longer this time.

"Okay—I'll leave the stuff at the reception desk. You can pick it up in the morning."

From the rustling sounds in the room, Nancy guessed that Wood was getting dressed again. He left his jacket in the closet, and a minute later, the room door opened.

Nancy waited until the key turned in the lock. Then she tiptoed out of the closet and ran toward the desk.

The documents were gone. Wood must have taken them to the reception desk.

There was a scratching noise at the window and George's head appeared.

"Pssst!" George hissed.

Nancy raised the window.

There was a rattle at the keyhole. Wood was coming back!

Nancy scrambled out the window and lowered herself onto the trash can.

"Hurry, Nan!" George gasped.

They bolted from the hotel yard. Keeping low, they made their way back to the car. Nancy got in the passenger's side and ducked down—Wood, if he came out, might recognize her. George got behind the wheel to drive back to the cabin.

"What'd you see?" George asked.

Nancy's eyes sparkled. "A lot," she said. "Wood has the stolen documents."

Back in the cabin, Nancy finished telling the adventure in the hotel room to Toby and Bess. Toby looked worried.

"Do you think Wood took the documents from me?" Toby said. "Is he a criminal, too?"

"Perhaps," Nancy said. "There's also a chance you gave Wood the documents."

"I don't believe that," Bess stated. "Toby never gave Wood the documents. He had to fight her for them. That's how she hurt her head and got amnesia. I say he stole them from her."

Nancy nodded. That could explain how Wood got that scratch on his face and why there was blood under Toby's fingernails. But there was no way of knowing.

"What's the next step?" George asked.

"The public library—first thing tomorrow morning," Nancy declared. "I want to read those newspaper articles that were on Wood's desk. I need to do a little research on paper mills."

"Can I help you at the library?" Toby asked.

Nancy smiled at her. "I think it's safer if you stay here," she said. "We don't want Wood—or the redheaded man—running into you. You stay here and rest. Bess can help me."

"Right. That's what I call a vacation," Bess grumbled.

"Hey, Nan!" Bess whispered. "Did you know that the Chinese invented paper about two thousand years ago? They found out that when you grind plants into pulp and dry the pulp flat, the fibers will bond together."

"I didn't know that," Nancy murmured. "What else have you dug up?"

It was now ten-thirty. Nancy and Bess had arrived at the library at nine, when it opened. Nancy had been looking through old issues of

93

the *Minosha Daily News* since then. Bess had been busy with encyclopedias, learning about paper mills and pollution.

Bess plunked herself into the chair next to Nancy. She waved her notes. "I found out that lots of paper mills today make pulp by boiling wood chips with chemicals. The chemical wastes are really bad."

Nancy nodded. "That's what these articles say, too," she said. "And there's more."

Bess leaned forward on her elbows. "Give me the scoop," she said.

"Well, it's kind of complicated," Nancy began. "The Minosha city government sold a big piece of lakefront property to the Castle family. The Castles wanted to build a paper mill on the land. A lot of people protested. They said the mill would pollute the lake. The people in WEB helped organize protests against building the mill. The whole town ended up divided over whether the mill would be good for Minosha."

"So what did the city government do?" asked Bess.

"Well, the mayor's office commissioned a study to see if the mill would be safe," Nancy explained. "All sorts of engineers and scientists were involved. The mayor had all their conclusions written up in a huge report. The report was given to the city council about three weeks ago."

"Let me guess—the report said building the mill would be okay," Bess said.

"That's right," Nancy answered. "It claimed the mill wouldn't pollute the lake."

"That must be the report Toby was working on," Bess said.

Nancy agreed. "There are two sides in this fight. No matter what the report said, one of those sides would be pretty unhappy."

Bess shivered. "Unhappy enough to hurt someone? Like Toby?" she asked.

"Maybe," Nancy answered. "And maybe one of them asked Toby to steal the documents the report was based on. If that's the case, the other side would be very angry with her."

"What about Mayor Castle?" Bess asked. "His family would own the mill. And as mayor he might be able to force the people of Minosha to accept the paper mill."

"It says here that he isn't involved in the family business," Nancy said. "When he was elected mayor he left the business so there wouldn't be a conflict of interest. His brother runs the business now."

Bess frowned thoughtfully. "But I'll bet the mayor isn't too far away."

Nancy stood up.

"Let's go, Bess," she said. "I want to talk to the reporter who covered the mill story. She might have more information—information that didn't make it into the newspaper articles."

But when they located the reporter—Laura Clark—she didn't have much to say. She didn't even seem very interested in the story she'd written.

"I can give you ten minutes," she said when Nancy explained why she and Bess were there. "Then I have to get back to work. I'm on a tight deadline."

Nancy didn't waste any time.

"We've heard rumors about the paper mill at the lake. Did the mayor's report tell the truth?"

Laura shrugged. "Reports always make people angry," she said. "This report is very complicated. But I think it told the truth."

"No one had doubts about it?" Nancy asked.

"One professor called me," Laura remembered. "He had some questions. He wasn't sure some facts were correct." She glanced at her watch.

"Do you remember his name?" Nancy asked.

Laura thought for a moment. Her mouth pursed.

"It began with an *F*," she said. "Ferranti, maybe."

"Arthur Ferranti?" Nancy asked.

"Right," said Laura. "Do you know him?"

"He's a professor at the University of Wisconsin," Nancy answered. "Did you answer his questions?"

"Some of them," Laura said. "But the paper mill was just one of the stories I was working on. I'm very busy. Which reminds me—I have to get back to work now."

Nancy and Bess stood up.

"Thanks for helping us," Nancy said.

"Who's Professor Ferranti?" Bess asked in the elevator.

"I found a big envelope from him on Donald Wood's desk," Nancy explained. "But it was empty."

"Do you think he sent Wood his questions about the mill?" Bess asked.

"Maybe," Nancy answered. "But why? If only we knew which side Wood is on. Is he Toby's friend—or her enemy?"

At the car, Bess stopped.

"Why don't I drive?" she asked. "You've done more than your share of driving in the past few days."

Nancy tossed Bess the keys, and the girls got into the car.

"Where to?" Bess adjusted the rearview mirror.

Nancy sighed.

"I'm trying to make up my mind. There are a few things I'd like to check here in town. But I really think we should talk to Toby first."

Bess looked at her watch.

"It's almost twelve," she said. "Why don't we go back to the cabin? We can talk to Toby and have lunch. You can come back to town later."

"Sounds good," Nancy said. "Maybe I'll even try to get in a swim before I come back."

Bess began backing out of the parking space.

There was a rumbling sound, and a van appeared out of nowhere. It hurtled down the aisle toward them at top speed.

"What's wrong with that driver?" Bess turned pale.

"Heads down!" Nancy yelled. "He's going to hit us!"

12

The Sooner the Better

With a sickening jolt, the van crashed into the back of Nancy's car.

The van veered away, careened around a corner, and vanished from the parking lot.

Nancy had been thrown against her seat belt so hard that she was having trouble breathing.

Bess was crumpled in the driver's seat. Her head rested on the steering wheel.

"Bess, are you all right?" Nancy was so short of breath she could barely speak.

Bess turned and stared at Nancy. Bess's face was white, and her whole body was shaking.

"That—that was too close," she said in a whisper.

"He could have hurt us if he had aimed a little closer," Nancy replied. "I think he was delivering a different message."

"'Mind your own business,' right?" Bess asked.

Nancy nodded.

Bess rubbed her forehead. "I'd rather get the message wrapped around a rock. Know what I mean?"

"I sure do," said Nancy. "I only wish I'd gotten a look at the driver," she added. "It's too late to chase him now."

"Did you see the license plate?" Bess asked.

Nancy frowned, trying to remember.

"I don't think there were any plates on the van," she said at last.

"Well, then, can we go back to the cabin?" Bess asked in a small voice. "I think I've had enough excitement for a while."

"Good idea. I'll drive if you'd like."

"I was hoping you'd say that," Bess said.

Nancy climbed out of the car. On her way around to the other side, she stopped to look at the rear fender.

"Nice job," she muttered angrily as she saw the deep dent and scratches. "Luckily I've got car insurance that'll cover that."

Nancy slid into the driver's seat.

The girls were silent on the drive back to

Aladdin's Cabins. They parked near the office and walked down the path through the woods.

"Don't say anything about the van to Toby," Nancy warned as they reached the cabin. "No sense in scaring her until we know more. She's nervous enough already."

"Hi," Toby greeted them. She was wearing George's bathrobe and drying her hair with a towel. "Two more minutes and there'll be fresh corn muffins coming hot from the oven."

She stared at the girls more closely.

"Everything okay? You look a little strange."

"Just hungry, I guess," Bess said.

She walked over to the oven. "I'll wait right here for those muffins." Bess was trying hard to be cheerful.

"Where's George?" Nancy asked.

"Swimming."

Toby looked suddenly serious. "She told me what happened in the hotel last night. I want to thank you, Nancy. I can't believe how brave you're being! And for the sake of a total stranger, too."

"Don't kid yourself," Bess remarked. "She's having a great time."

Nancy smiled. "Did anything George told you strike a chord in your memory?"

Toby brightened.

"Yes! The paper mill. I know hundreds of

101

facts about paper mills. I must have studied them."

"I think we know why," Nancy said.

She and Bess told Toby everything they'd learned that morning.

"Arthur Ferranti." Toby looked thoughtful. "Hey, I know that name! Maybe I studied with him."

"Why don't we try calling him at the university?" Nancy suggested. "He might be able to clear everything up."

But after a few minutes on the phone, she hung up with a frustrated sigh.

"I only got an answering machine," she told Bess and Toby. "He's away on vacation. The message didn't say when he'd be back."

"Maybe someone else at the university could help us," Toby said, taking the golden brown muffins from the oven.

"No," Nancy said. "Everything seems to be happening in Minosha. That's where I think we'll find all our answers."

Nancy picked up two of the hot muffins.

"And speaking of Minosha, I think I'll skip lunch and head back to town. I want to talk to Sandy Lauffer and the mayor again," she said. "I want to see exactly where the mayor stands on this paper mill business."

"Want me to come with you?" Bess asked, trying to be brave.

"No, that's okay." Nancy smiled. "It's a one-person job. You just get some sun. And some food," Nancy said, biting into a muffin.

Inside Town Hall, Nancy went straight to room 112—the records department, where Sandy Lauffer worked. A man she hadn't seen before told her that Sandy would be back from lunch any minute.

Sandy Lauffer walked through the door about five minutes later. When she saw Nancy, her eyes widened and she stopped in the doorway. Nancy was sure she would have turned and walked away if Nancy hadn't already seen her.

"Hello," Nancy said. "We spoke yesterday. I've gotten some more information since then. Do you have a few minutes to talk?"

Sandy glanced nervously down the hall.

"Okay," she said after a second. "But come into my back office."

Sandy led Nancy into a small, windowless room and closed the door behind them.

"Now, what is it you want to talk about?" she asked. She sounded guarded.

"I found out that Toby was working on that

big report about the new paper mill," Nancy said. "I hear some people think the report isn't true."

Sandy looked startled.

"I'm sure the mayor wouldn't release a false report," Sandy said, sounding angry. "Mayor Castle has always done a good job."

"It may not be his fault," Nancy answered. "It's a complicated report. Lots of people worked on it. For instance—have you ever heard the name Donald Wood?"

Sandy shook her head no.

"How about Arthur Ferranti?" Nancy asked.

Sandy shook her head again. "Neither of them worked on the report," she said. "I do a good job, Nancy. But I wouldn't get involved in anything wrong."

"I understand," Nancy said. "And I'm sure this whole situation will be cleared up soon. Could you tell me one more thing? Who is allowed to see city documents?"

"Only Town Hall employees, with permission," Sandy answered. "You have to get a signed permission form from this office."

"And did Toby have a form?" Nancy asked.

Sandy paused. Then, in a low voice, she said, "I think she faked the signature on the form to get those documents."

"I see." Nancy stood up to go. "Thank you for your time."

Sandy looked frightened. "Where are you going now?" she asked.

"To talk to Mayor Castle," Nancy said. "But don't worry, Sandy. You haven't given anything away."

Nancy smiled as she headed to the second floor, where the mayor's office was. Sandy had told her one thing—neither Donald Wood nor Arthur Ferranti had worked on the paper mill report.

As she rounded the corner at the landing, Nancy heard voices. She peered down at the end of the hall. Two men were talking there.

The minute she recognized them, Nancy backed out of sight. One man was Donald Wood; the other was the mayor.

Nancy leaned against the wall. She strained to catch what they were saying. But she could only hear occasional words.

". . . She's still missing . . ." said Donald Wood.

He must be talking about Toby! Nancy thought.

The mayor sounded angry. "Not missing— hiding!" he said. There was something Nancy didn't catch—and then, "under arrest."

Suddenly Mayor Castle raised his voice. And this time Nancy heard every syllable.

"This would all be a lot easier," he exclaimed, "without strangers playing detective. They're the ones I'd like to get rid of. And the sooner the better."

13

Follow That Ferry!

As quietly as she could, Nancy started down the stairs.

"I'll see you later," she heard Mayor Castle say. A door slammed.

Footsteps, probably Wood's, started down the stairs, one flight behind Nancy.

Nancy reached the last step and darted silently into the first-floor corridor. She slipped into an open doorway and turned her back to the hall. The footsteps passed her.

Nancy peered down the hall in time to see Wood stride across the lobby of Town Hall and out the main entrance.

Nancy followed Wood down to High Street.

He didn't notice her on the busy street, but Nancy had to work not to lose him among the passersby.

Wood didn't slow down for a second. He was in a hurry to get somewhere.

Near the end of the street, Nancy suddenly realized he was heading for the ferry.

She began walking faster, too. This time she didn't want to have to jump aboard.

Wood stopped at the ticket booth and handed over a crumpled bill. He tapped his keys on the counter as he waited for his change. Then he turned and walked to the very end of the ferry dock. He stared out to sea.

Nancy paid for her ticket. Wood suddenly turned and glanced in her direction.

Nancy stepped back into the shadow of the ticket booth. Her pulse was racing—but Wood hadn't recognized her. He seemed to be searching for someone else.

After a few seconds he gave up and stared out to sea again.

"That was close," Nancy muttered to herself.

The ferry pulled in. Its whistle blew twice, and the people waiting on the dock began gathering up their things.

"All aboard!" called the conductor.

Wood was the first passenger onto the ferry. Nancy followed as closely as she dared.

Wood walked to the back of the boat. He took a chair on the open deck. Nancy took one safely off to the side behind him.

"First stop—Little Isle." The conductor's cheerful voice came over the loudspeaker.

Wood paid no attention. He was scanning a newspaper he'd brought aboard with him.

Nancy couldn't help smiling. This guy was a complete newspaper fanatic.

She wished she could walk right up to Wood and start a conversation. She might find out why the mayor wanted to get rid of people who play detective. Did he mean Nancy? Or Toby? Or both?

"Little Isle!" the conductor announced again.

The ferry slowed down, then stopped.

Wood glanced up from his newspaper. But he made no move to get off the ferry.

Nancy wondered what stop they were waiting for.

Wood nodded. It was just a tiny movement of his head—but it was definitely a signal.

Nancy glanced in the direction Wood was looking. A man stood near the entrance to the deck. He wore sunglasses and a boating hat that was pulled way down.

Without looking at Wood, he moved into the shade on the opposite side of the deck. Wood stared at him for a second, then went back to his paper.

The man standing in the shade pulled off his sunglasses, then his cap. Nancy inhaled sharply. It was the redheaded man.

Nancy sat far back in her seat. She was afraid that he would notice her so she sat as quietly as she could.

"Lido! Next stop!" the conductor called.

Neither Wood nor the Peeping Tom moved. Five minutes passed. Nancy fidgeted in her chair. The view of the shore from the ferry was lovely, but she was too impatient to enjoy it.

"Last stop! Grand Isle!" called the conductor.

Everyone still left on the ferry moved toward the front of the boat.

Wood and the red-haired man reached the ferry door at the same time. Without speaking, they fell into step next to each other and strode down the ferry ramp.

Nancy was right behind them. She followed them down the ramp toward what seemed to be Grand Isle's main street.

It was a beautiful street—even prettier than High Street in Minosha. The gleaming store windows were filled with luxuries—jewelry, expensive clothes, and fancy foods.

At the end of the block, the street curved. Now there were only houses—stately Victorian homes on lush lawns.

But Nancy couldn't pay much attention to the scenery. She was too busy trying to keep Wood and the Peeping Tom in sight without letting them see her.

The two men walked on opposite sides of the street.

Wood turned up a narrow road. The red-haired man followed.

The houses on this new road were even bigger and were set even farther apart. No one was walking outside, except the two men and Nancy. There was no way Nancy could hide in a crowd now.

Up ahead, Wood made another turn. The red-haired man followed after him.

Nancy came to the spot where the two men had turned off. A curving dirt road ran through a wooded area.

She walked briskly up the dirt road. At the first bend she caught sight of the two men. Then they vanished around another bend.

But when Nancy reached the second bend, the two men had disappeared.

"What on earth—" Nancy muttered. "I can't lose them now!"

A high barbed-wire fence ran along the road at the edge of the woods. Could the men have climbed over it?

A sign was posted on the fence a few feet ahead:

PRIVATE PROPERTY

TRESPASSERS WILL BE PROSECUTED

Next to the sign, the barbed wire had been carefully snipped, leaving an opening just wide enough for a person to slip through.

Determined not to lose the two men, Nancy pulled the wire back and slipped through the opening. On the other side, she found a narrow path through the trees.

Moving as silently as possible, she followed the path. The woods were quiet. A bird screamed once, then fell silent.

After a few minutes the path suddenly ended in a clearing.

Nancy found herself at the edge of an immense, perfectly groomed lawn. Tall bushes hid her from sight.

She took a close look around. She was in back of a redbrick mansion. A marble terrace stretched from the back of the mansion to an oval swimming pool.

Umbrella tables and lawn chairs were scattered around the pool. Flower boxes and wicker rockers lined the terrace. Not far from Nancy stood a greenhouse, and to one side was an old-fashioned carriage house.

"Nice little country place," Nancy murmured. She surveyed the scene. There was no sign of Wood or the redheaded man.

Nancy ran closer. She hid behind the greenhouse and peered around the corner.

There was still no one in sight. The vast emerald lawn was empty.

As Nancy watched, the back door of the brick house swung open. A woman about fifty years old stepped out. She wore a blue silk dress and held a vase of lilies.

She carried the vase over to a glass table on the terrace. She began rearranging the lilies in the vase.

A telephone rang somewhere in the house. A moment later, a man in a butler's uniform walked out of the back door and up to the woman in blue.

"Mrs. Castle, your husband's on the telephone," he said.

Mrs. Castle! Nancy gasped. It was the mayor's house. What were Wood and the redhead doing there?

113

"Thank you, Jeffrey," Mrs. Castle said to the butler. She moved toward the house.

Nancy heard a twig snap behind her.

A moment later a pair of strong arms grabbed her from behind.

They closed like a vise around her neck.

14

No Trespassing

"What are you doing here?" a low voice growled in Nancy's ear. "This is private property!"

"N-nothing!" Nancy choked. "Nothing at all. I'm a tourist and—and I got lost."

The strong arms spun her around. Nancy was face-to-face with a burly security guard.

"Right," the guard sneered. "A tourist who cuts through a barbed-wire fence. Then snoops around private property."

"I didn't cut the fence," Nancy protested. "I was only trying to find the main road."

"Sure," the guard snapped. "Try telling that to the mayor. Let's go!"

His grip on Nancy's arm was painfully tight. He walked her toward the house.

Mrs. Castle appeared at the back door. "What's the problem, Ralph?"

"I caught this girl spying on you," the guard answered.

"I'm sorry if I trespassed," Nancy said. "I was lost. If you'd just let me explain . . ."

Mrs. Castle eyed her coolly. "We have a lot of trouble with tourists."

"We should teach this one a lesson," the guard insisted.

"I suppose so," Mrs. Castle sighed. "Maybe they'll know what to do at the police station. Ralph, would you please call the police?"

"Just what I was on my way to do, Mrs. Castle."

Ralph turned to Nancy. He jerked his head toward the house.

"That way," he said. He yanked Nancy toward a side entrance into the house.

"Not so rough!" Nancy said angrily. "I won't run away, you know."

Mrs. Castle gazed after Nancy. Her lips pursed.

"You can let go of her, Ralph," she said at last.

"Thank you." Nancy straightened her clothes. Her arm ached where the guard had

116

grabbed her. She brushed a dead leaf off her shirt.

"I'd like to call someone, too," Nancy said. "His name's Richard Banner, and he works for the mayor."

"Sure—call him. Call whoever you want," Ralph said. "After I make my call."

The guard led Nancy into the kitchen, where he punched a number on the wall phone.

"Hey, Smithy," he said into the receiver. "It's Brady. Picked up a trespasser on the Castle property. Can you take her off my hands?"

In a few moments he hung up and turned to Nancy.

"The police will be here in half an hour," he said.

"May I make my call?"

"Be my guest." Ralph spoke with mock politeness.

Nancy looked through her purse. Where was the slip of paper with Richard Banner's phone number? Finally she found it and dialed.

Banner picked up after two rings. "Mayor's office—special projects," he said.

"Richard, it's Nancy Drew. Remember me?"

"Nancy! Of course. What can I do for you?"

"Well, you're not going to believe this,"

Nancy said. She told him what had happened, leaving out the fact that she'd been following the two men.

Ralph was listening closely, so Nancy stuck to her story—she'd simply been sightseeing and had taken what she thought was an interesting path. She'd never meant to trespass.

Banner promised to come help straighten things out.

Banner arrived at the house at the same time as the police officers.

"They let me ride on the boat with them," Banner explained. "I'll talk to Mrs. Castle right away."

"Thanks," Nancy said gratefully. "Do you want me to come with you?"

"Oh, no, you don't," Ralph told her. "You're going to stay right here and answer Lieutenant Dougherty's questions."

For the next five minutes Nancy did her best to convince the lieutenant that she hadn't done anything wrong.

She was relieved to see Richard Banner come back with a smile on his face.

"All set," he said cheerfully. "I'll just escort you off the property, and then you're free."

Nancy thought Ralph looked disappointed.

Banner led her back to the police boat.

Nancy breathed a sigh of relief. "Thanks a million," she said. "I appreciate it. But how did you manage to spring me?"

Richard Banner grinned. "Oh, I told Mrs. Castle that you were just an overly enthusiastic tourist. I guaranteed that you weren't out to steal the silver tea set or the jewels. There won't be any charges."

Banner helped Nancy climb into the police boat.

"I hate to do it," he said, "but I have to give you a little lecture. Be a good kid and listen. I want you to promise that you won't go trespassing anymore. I can't have you ruining my reputation at Town Hall."

"Don't worry," Nancy said firmly. "I'll stay out of trouble from now on."

She leaned back in the boat. The wind streamed through her hair, and she tried to enjoy the ride and the beautiful day.

The forty-eight hours of silence she had promised Toby were up. And the solution to Toby's mystery was still out of reach.

Toby needed to see a doctor. The rest of the case would have to wait. As soon as she got back to the cabin, Nancy would take Toby to the hospital herself.

There was a grinding sound as the police boat pulled up to the main dock in Minosha.

Nancy was surprised at how fast the trip had been.

She turned to Richard Banner.

"I guess I haven't been very good company," she apologized. "But thank you for getting me out of trouble."

"Hey, no problem."

Banner climbed out of the boat. "Do you need a lift anywhere?"

"I'm parked near the high school," Nancy said. "It's an easy walk."

Banner grinned. "Not that easy. It'll take twenty minutes to walk there."

Nancy paused. A ride would be nice, she thought. And certainly faster.

"Okay," she agreed. "I'd appreciate a ride."

Banner's face lit up. "Great! Come on."

As they walked toward Banner's car, Nancy suddenly remembered the question she'd been meaning to ask him.

She pulled the WEB button out of her purse. "Is this button yours, by any chance?"

Banner shook his head. "I know that group," he said. "But the button's not mine. What made you think it was?"

"We found it outside our cabin after you left yesterday," Nancy explained. "I thought you might have dropped it."

"Nope. Maybe it belongs to that Peeping Tom," Banner suggested.

"Maybe." Nancy was doubtful. "But he wasn't on the porch—which is where we found the button. Though he could have sneaked all around the cabin before we saw him."

"A lovely thought," Banner joked. "There's my car—across the street."

He pointed to a gleaming white convertible. He led Nancy to it and helped her in. Then he got into the driver's seat.

Nancy noticed that the car still smelled new. It seemed like a very expensive car for an assistant to the mayor of a small town.

"Phew—hot day, isn't it?" Banner took off his jacket and threw it into the backseat. "Too hot for a coat and tie. Or a top." Banner flipped a switch and the white convertible top began to fold back.

"By the way"—Banner paused—"how's Toby Jackson doing?"

"Oh, she's much better, but . . ."

Nancy froze. She had just given herself—and Toby—away.

Richard Banner stared at her.

"So you do know where she is." He flashed Nancy a crooked smile. "I thought so."

Nancy couldn't speak. She was furious with herself. After all the care she'd taken, she had just let out Toby's secret. Nancy felt miserable.

"Richard, I know it must seem strange, but Toby hasn't done anything wrong. I'm sure of it."

"Oh, I believe you," he said.

Nancy started to thank him. She glanced at his bare arm in surprise.

His arm was covered with long, angry-looking scratches.

"Pretty awful looking, isn't it?" he said easily. "My next-door neighbor has a German shepherd pup that hasn't been trained yet. He thinks he's playing—and I wind up looking as though I've been in combat."

"When did it happen?" Nancy asked.

"A few days ago." Banner pulled into traffic. "I'll have to be more careful next time."

Nancy nodded. "Puppies are cute, but they can play rough," she agreed.

Banner's explanation sounded logical, but Nancy felt suddenly uneasy. Something in his manner made her think he was lying.

"Make a left turn at the next block," Nancy said. "My car's at the end of School Street."

She hoped she sounded normal.

"Yes, there's my car," she said a moment

later. Her hand was already on the door handle. "That blue one up there."

Nancy had the door open even before the car had stopped moving.

"Thanks a lot." Quickly, Nancy unfastened her seat belt. "I'll talk to you soon. It was nice of you to . . ."

Inside the edge of the passenger door was a scrap of pink fabric. Nancy recognized it instantly.

It was fabric from Toby's shirt.

15

Prisoner!

"What's the matter, Nancy?" Banner asked in a quiet voice. "You look like you've seen a ghost."

"No, it's nothing. I—I just remembered that my friends expected me back at the cabin for lunch. They'll be wondering where I am. I'd better hurry home."

Nancy started to open the car door all the way. But before she could get out, Banner leaned across in front of her and pulled it shut again. She heard the automatic locks click on both doors at the same time. It would be impossible to unlock them without pushing the release button by Banner's side.

"You'd better let me drive you back to the cabin," Banner said. "I think we have some important things to straighten out."

Nancy sat helplessly as he put the car in gear and drove on down the street, leaving her own car far behind.

The drive to Aladdin's Cabins had never seemed so long. Banner drove in silence, as though he no longer had any interest in his prisoner.

Of course not, Nancy told herself as she gazed straight ahead at the highway, dim in the pink glow of sunset. It was Toby he was after. She shook her head in disgust. She had actually trusted him. Now Toby would pay for Nancy's mistake.

Please be out somewhere, Nancy silently willed her friends. Don't let Banner walk into the cabin and take you by surprise!

About five miles out of town, Banner suddenly pulled the car over to a small gas station beside the highway.

"Stay here," he said to Nancy. His stern voice was very different from his normal one. "I'll be right back."

He got out of the car, taking the keys with him. Nancy watched as he greeted the teen-aged boy who came out to gas up the car.

Now's your chance, she told herself. Do it!

While Banner leaned against her side of the car, waiting for the station attendant to finish filling the gas tank, Nancy slid very slowly across the front seat toward the driver's side. There were about twenty inches to the driver's door. Then fifteen. Then twelve.

Nancy glanced nervously over her shoulder. Banner was leaning against her car door with his back to her. He hadn't noticed that Nancy was trying to escape.

Quietly, Nancy eased the driver's door open. Banner was reaching to take his wallet out of his pocket to pay for the gas. She slipped noiselessly out onto the cement driveway. Squatting, she edged toward the highway.

Once on the road, she could run into the woods and hide until Banner gave up looking for her. Then she could call their cabin and warn Toby.

She reached the edge of the driveway. Banner finished paying the attendant and turned to get back into the car. He saw Nancy.

She sprang forward, but Banner leapt after her.

"Let me go," Nancy cried.

"Think you can get away, eh?"

Banner grabbed her arm and pulled her back toward the car. Nancy looked wildly

126

around for the attendant, but he had gone back into the station and was nowhere in sight.

"Your friend Toby tried the same thing." Banner's handsome face twisted with anger.

"She tried to jump out of the car while we were driving. She almost made me wreck my car, trying to keep her still. I ran into a tree. Served her right—she was pitched into the windshield. I don't know how she got away from me. I was sure I'd broken half my ribs."

Banner pushed Nancy back into the car.

"You were with Toby then?" Nancy was surprised. "She was badly hurt."

"And you'd better watch it, if you don't want the same thing to happen to you," Banner said. His voice was cold.

Banner started the engine. He pulled onto the highway with his tires squealing.

"So Toby told you everything," Banner said. His lips were tight. "Well, I'm not worried. I'll stop her before she tells anyone else. No one will believe Toby, anyway."

Nancy looked at him out of the corner of her eye. One thing was certainly clear. Banner was a very dangerous man.

She would have to outsmart Richard Banner.

"Well, this is an interesting development," she said, forcing her voice to stay steady. "I guess this means that Mayor Castle is involved in the paper mill project after all. Even though he promised not to involve himself in any business dealings while he was in office."

She glanced at Banner. "That's a conflict of interest," she added. "And if he put false information in the report—that's fraud. He could go to jail."

"The mayor's not stupid," Banner sneered, keeping his eyes on the road. "There's a lot going on in Minosha these days. Why should a man like Castle deal himself out? He's too smart a businessman for that."

He turned to grin at Nancy. "He's also too smart to leave any evidence of fraud."

"But the paper mill could destroy the lake," Nancy said. "It would ruin the tourist industry."

Banner laughed at Nancy. "The mayor doesn't care about the lake—or about the tourists. He's a rich man, and he wants to get richer."

Sadly, Nancy shook her head. "And he'd destroy his own town to get richer. He must be a very greedy man," she said.

"He's a very smart man." Banner gave Nancy a dirty look. "And no little snoop like you is going to stop him. That mill's going to be built—no matter what some stupid report says."

Nancy's eyes narrowed. "Then the real report said the mill should never be built. And Mayor Castle made a fake report to make sure his plan would be voted in."

"Pretty clever, Miss Drew. You're not as dumb as you look. Too bad you won't be around to get even smarter."

Nancy ignored his threats. She eyed the sleek, shiny car that Banner seemed so proud of. "The mayor pays you well, too, doesn't he?" she said.

"That he does." Banner gave Nancy a sharp look as he turned onto the narrow road leading to Aladdin's Cabins.

"Let me tell you something I've learned from the mayor, Nancy Drew. Money talks. Castle will do anything to get that paper mill built here in Minosha. It's guaranteed to make him another fortune. He won't deal kindly with anyone who tries to get in his way."

Nancy frowned. "Tell me one thing. The redheaded man—the Peeping Tom—is he one of Mayor Castle's special 'assistants,' too?" she asked. "And what about Donald Wood?"

"Wood?" Banner parked the car in front of the office and turned off the engine. "Never heard of him. And as for your Peeping Tom, he was probably just hoping to rob your cabin. We've got some small-time thieves around Minosha."

"So I see," Nancy said grimly.

Banner unlocked Nancy's door and reached past her to open it. "Let's go to your cabin. And don't think about calling for help."

Nancy glanced toward the office cabin. There was a faint light in the window. Surely Mr. Wickman was inside. But Nancy didn't dare make a sound. Too clearly, she remembered the bruises on Toby's arms.

Banner pushed her from behind. "Get going," he growled.

As she stumbled along the dark, narrow path in front of Banner, Nancy tried to piece together the mystery. If Wood and the red-haired man weren't part of the mayor's scheme, they were on Toby's side, trying to help her. It made sense now. The red-haired man grabbing Bess in the woods, spying on their cabin—he was trying to find Toby to protect her. And the papers in Donald Wood's hotel room—Toby had probably risked great danger to get the papers to him. Nancy's cheeks flamed. She had suspected the wrong men!

The aroma of supper cooking wafted from the cabin windows. The cabin looked warm

and cheerful. But Nancy's friends looked anything but cheerful when Nancy entered. And
no wonder. Banner was twisting Nancy's arm
painfully behind her back.

"What's happened?" George cried. She
rushed toward Nancy.

"Stay back!" Banner commanded. "If any
one of you comes near me, this snoop really
gets hurt!"

"Banner's the one who hurt Toby," Nancy
gasped out. "He tried to get the real report's
support documents from her. She fought him,
he lost control of his car and ran into the tree
by the highway. Toby's head hit the windshield
—that's why she has amnesia."

"Amnesia?" Banner stared at Toby. The
young woman was pale and trembling.

"You mean we were scared of her—for nothing?" Banner was really angry. "Do you expect
me to believe that?"

"No—because I remember now," Toby said.
She stared at Banner with wide eyes. "I was
scratching at him, trying to get away."

"That's right." Banner's eyes blazed. "And
you made me run my car right off the highway.
I should make you pay for the damage."

"Look, Mr. Banner." Bess stood with a soup
spoon held over a pot on the stove. "Just tell us
what you want in return for Nancy's safety. We

131

haven't got any documents, if that's what you're looking for."

Banner grinned at Bess. "All I want in exchange for Miss Drew is"—he nodded toward Toby—"all I want is her!"

"That's right."

Everyone turned at the sound of the deep voice. Mayor Castle was standing in the doorway.

Behind him stood Ralph, the security guard. Ralph glared at Nancy. Mrs. Castle must have told her husband about her trespassing, Nancy realized.

She remembered now that Banner had spoken in private to Mrs. Castle. Nancy groaned.

"Banner, let Miss Drew go," Mayor Castle said in a cool, clipped voice.

Banner scowled, but he backed away from Nancy. She rubbed her arm gingerly.

"Now, ladies, let's not make this more unpleasant than we have to," the mayor said. He nodded to Ralph, who strode over to Toby. He stood next to her, ready to stop her from running away.

"We have here a simple case of theft," Mayor Castle said. "Toby's a bright young woman. I personally chose her for the summer intern program. But she got involved in matters over her head. She stole important papers from my office. The law is pretty strict about stealing, even in a small place like Minosha."

"But I didn't steal anything," Toby cried. "I'm sure I didn't!"

The mayor frowned, as though considering what she'd said. "Of course," he said slowly. "I understand that young people can sometimes make foolish mistakes. Maybe you misplaced the documents. Or took them home by mistake."

He lifted his pale eyes to meet Toby's.

"I'll tell you what," he said. "If you'll hand over the papers now, and promise not to mention them again, we'll let you all leave Minosha without any trouble. Now, does that sound fair enough?"

"But I don't have them," Toby insisted. "I don't remember—I don't even remember what they said."

"That's right," Nancy said quickly. "Toby was in a bad car accident. She hit her head on the windshield and has had amnesia ever since. But she's starting to remember things now. Maybe she'll be able to lead you to the papers and then you can let her go."

It was a gamble, but it was the only plan Nancy could think of. If the mayor thought that

Toby could help him, he wouldn't hurt her. At least not until he had his hands on the stolen papers.

The trick was to buy enough time to figure out what to do.

"That's ridiculous," George said hotly. "Toby didn't steal anything. Mayor Castle's just worried about getting in hot water over his paper mill scam!"

"Yeah," Bess chimed in, waving her spoon. "Toby's as innocent as I am. And I'll bet Nancy can prove it. She's a great detective. She's solved lots of cases tougher than this one!"

Mayor Castle, Ralph, and Banner all turned to stare at Nancy.

Nancy's heart sank.

16

Out to Lake Minosha

Mayor Castle broke the silence in the room.

"You think you can save Toby? And frighten me?" The mayor laughed.

"You heard the girls," Banner said to the mayor. "Nancy Drew is a detective. And she's been on our trail since she came to Minosha. Maybe she won't give up until she's nailed us. We should take her, too."

"No, don't!" Toby cried before Nancy could say anything. "I'll show you where the documents are. I promise! Just leave these girls alone. All they did was take care of me. They don't know anything."

"Yes, we do," Bess retorted hotly.

Too late, Bess realized how dangerous her words sounded. She covered her mouth with her hand.

Castle glanced at his assistant, then looked at Nancy again.

"No," he said at last. "Even if Miss Drew tried to expose us, it would be her word against mine. Without Toby or the papers, no one will listen to a word she says. Who's going to take a tourist's word over a Castle's in this town?"

He turned toward the door. "Come on," he said to Ralph and Banner. "Young Toby here has offered to return our property to us. Let's go get it."

They started to leave. Nancy had never felt so helpless. There was nothing she could do to stop them.

The front door burst open, almost knocking Ralph over. Two men raced into the room.

"The Peeping Tom!" George gasped. "And Donald Wood!"

"What are they doing here?" the mayor cried.

"Good question," Banner said. "Who are you, anyway?"

The redhead ignored Banner and went up to Mayor Castle.

"It's a pleasure meeting you, Mayor, after so

long. I feel I know you well. My name is Arthur Ferranti."

"Arthur Ferranti." Toby stared at the redhead with wide eyes. "I think I remember—"

"The professor," Bess said. "The one who wrote to the newspaper about the mistakes in the report!"

Ferranti turned to her, surprised. Then he turned back to the mayor. "Toby Jackson is a student of mine. We worked in the ecology program at the university in Madison. If anything happens to her, you'll regret it."

"Forget the tough talk," Banner snapped. He turned to Wood. "Sorry, but I don't know who you are, either."

Wood grinned wryly at Nancy. "Donald Wood," he said. "I'm a reporter in Madison. Arthur turned me on to this paper mill scam. I was about to break the story—and break it big. But when Toby disappeared, we had to postpone the story. We wanted Toby safe first."

"Your story's going to be permanently postponed, my friend." The mayor gave him a cold smile. "The young lady made a deal with us. The documents are already ours."

"Yours and everyone else's," Wood said loudly. "You lied to the people who elected you. Everyone's going to know that soon. Why

137

make things worse for yourself by adding kidnapping to your list of crimes?"

The mayor sighed. "This is no kidnapping. The young lady broke the law. She took some confidential papers from my office. Now we're offering her the chance to return them."

"We'll see what the people of Minosha think about that—when they read it in the papers," Wood said.

The mayor shook his head at the young man. "You're a stranger here," he said. "So you may not realize this. The Minosha newspaper is owned by the Castle family. It's not likely to print an unkind word about me."

Wood stared at the mayor. He seemed at a loss for words.

Nancy had a strong feeling that Wood and Ferranti were trying to stall for time.

Mayor Castle must have felt the same thing. He turned suddenly to Ralph and ordered him out the door.

"Wait." Wood moved between Ralph and the door. Ferranti stepped beside Wood.

Ralph let go of Toby and charged into Donald Wood. The reporter reeled against the wall of the cabin. Ferranti jumped at Ralph. He threw his arms around the guard. Ralph threw him off easily. Ferranti landed on the floor with a thud.

138

"Ralph," the mayor yelled, "leave them alone. Get Toby—get the girl."

The guard's eyes opened wide. He didn't seem to understand.

"Go after her!" the mayor shouted. "Toby is gone!"

Bess bent over Ferranti, trying to help. Banner, Mayor Castle, and Ralph ran onto the porch together.

"That way!" The mayor pointed toward the woods. "Surround her!"

"We've got to save Toby," Nancy said the moment the men were gone.

She helped George lift Donald Wood to his feet. Ferranti had already stood up.

"Come on," Nancy told them all. "Castle thinks he owns this town, that he can do whatever he wants. We have to rescue Toby. He won't go easy on her."

They ran down the front steps of the porch. In the distance they could hear Mayor Castle and Banner shouting.

"She must have gone toward the lake," Nancy said in a low voice. "It's easier to run there, without the trees."

"We'll run out in the woods and meet on the shore, then." Ferranti ran to the back of the house.

"Bess, you stay here in case Toby doubles

139

back," Nancy ordered. "If she does, take her to Mr. Wickman's office and call the police."

Nancy raced after Ferranti. Wood and George were close behind.

It was hard going, running through the woods in the dark of night. Branches slashed Nancy's face and snatched at her clothes. Once she tripped over a rock and landed facedown in the leaves.

But she got up quickly and kept running toward the lake. Toby's life might be at stake. And Nancy would never forget how Toby had put herself in danger to save Nancy and her friends.

A short distance to the right, Nancy could hear Ferranti running through the trees. When she reached the shore of the lake, he was already there.

George and Donald arrived just after Nancy. They stood on the shore for a moment, staring at something in the moonlight.

"It's them!" George said.

It was hard to see in the darkness. But three people stood on the shore.

"Banner and Ralph have Toby!" Ferranti said.

Before the others could move, he ran toward her.

"Banner!" Ferranti shouted as he approached the men. "Ralph! She hasn't got the documents—I have."

Banner and Ralph peered into the darkness. Nancy noticed Mayor Castle coming through the woods. He stood by his men.

"Where are they?" Castle demanded.

"In a safe place," Ferranti said. His voice trembled. "Let go of Toby, and I'll take you there."

"If you don't let her go, you can read about it on the front page of tomorrow's paper. I'll see to that," Wood shouted.

Ralph looked worried.

"The professor's lying," Banner said. He gestured at Toby. "She said the same thing— that she knew where the documents were— when she thought it would help her get away."

"Stop this before it's too late," Ferranti pleaded. "You haven't done much yet. The police won't go easy on a kidnapping charge— or worse."

"Police?" Banner laughed. "Forget the police!" Banner pulled out a gun and waved it at Ferranti, Wood, George, and Nancy. "What are the police going to do to me?"

"They're going to arrest you, Banner," a voice said from the shadows.

141

A flashlight was switched on at the edge of the woods where a path led to Mr. Wickman's office. The flashlight was held by a police officer. In his other hand he held a pistol.

"Drop the gun," he said to Banner. Three more police officers appeared. Then Bess stepped out of the woods.

17

All the Pieces in Place

Banner dropped the gun. Toby ran to join Nancy, Bess, and George.

"Bess!" Nancy exclaimed. "Am I glad to see you—and the police. But what happened? I thought you were waiting at the cabin."

Bess nodded. "I know—but I couldn't stay there. I was too worried about all of you. So I went to the office and called the police."

"We got here as quickly as possible," a police officer told Nancy. "Your friend said the mayor committed a crime."

"And you said you had proof," another officer said. "You understand, we can't arrest the mayor without plenty of proof."

143

"Right here, Officer." Donald Wood pulled a sheaf of papers from the inside of his jacket. He held them out and a police officer shone his flashlight beam on them.

The other police officer flipped through the papers.

"The documents," George said to Nancy. "Wood had them all the time."

"But, Mayor," a voice said. "It's police policy."

They all turned to see a young police officer standing in front of the mayor, holding up a pair of handcuffs. The mayor had taken a step back and was refusing to put them on.

The older officer joined them.

"Mayor Castle," he said in a weary voice. "Put on the handcuffs. From what I've seen, you're going to be wearing them for a long, long time."

"I still have a lot of questions," Wood said to Nancy.

"Well, this time try asking me," Toby said, her eyes shining. "I'm starting to remember things now. And I've got a lot to tell."

The next afternoon, Nancy hurried to join George and Bess on the porch of the cabin. George had her legs propped up on the porch railing, and Bess was stretched out on a lounge chair.

"At last," George cried.

"It's four o'clock," Bess said, glancing at her watch. She sat up. "What took you so long? You left at eight-thirty this morning. I hope everything's okay."

"There was a lot to do," Nancy reminded her. "We all had to appear before the judge. It took hours to explain everything. And Toby did have to go to the hospital for a checkup."

"Is she okay now?" George asked.

"Fine," Nancy assured her. "She promised to get a ride over here as soon as she could."

Bess stood and walked to the cabin door. "I'm getting something to munch on while we wait. Want anything?"

"I'll have a few of your taco chips," George said. "I'm getting to like them—sort of."

Bess returned with a bag of taco chips, a pitcher of lemonade, and some glasses.

"I guess I didn't realize how hard it must be to put a mayor in jail," she said.

George nodded. "Last night, it was everyone's word against Mayor Castle's. We're lucky that Donald had those documents with him."

"And that some of the police were already suspicious of Banner and the mayor," Nancy added.

She reached for the lemonade and spotted Toby walking up the path. Nancy grinned at their new friend.

"Judging from the way you look, I'd say there hasn't been a disaster," she said.

"Far from it," Toby said with a smile. "Thanks to all of you."

Bess picked up a taco chip, held it high in front of her, and declared, "Here's to the end of a mystery. Cheers!" She bit into the taco chip.

"So what happened?" George asked. "Let's hear all the nitty-gritty details."

Toby sat on the porch steps. "I'm much better," she said. "The shock of seeing Banner, Arthur, and Donald again helped my memory a lot. The doctor wants to keep a close watch on me. But he said I'm going to be fine."

"And now for the other nitty-gritty?" Bess asked.

"Well, the big news," Nancy began, "is that Banner and Mayor Castle gave complete confessions."

"This morning?" George asked.

Nancy nodded. "It turns out that Mayor Castle had forced Sandy Lauffer to alter many of the statements in the report. He threatened to have her fired without her pension if she didn't cooperate. Sandy made the report say that the mill wouldn't hurt the lake or local wildlife."

"Would it have been really bad for the lake?" Bess asked.

"Terrible!" Nancy said. "The Castles weren't going to put in any of the necessary safeguards. That would have cut into their profits."

"And Banner got a share of the whole deal," George guessed.

"Right," Nancy said. "The project was in his name. He was in charge of the phony report. Mayor Castle had promised to make him a rich man."

"Then what happened?" Bess asked.

"Then Toby realized what was going on. She took the documents supporting the real report and called her friend Arthur Ferranti. He came up from Madison to go over them."

"And Arthur got in touch with the reporter, Donald Wood," Toby added.

"So the mayor had Toby kidnapped," Nancy went on. "It was pretty risky, but Mayor Castle knew a fortune was at stake. He was hoping to scare Toby into giving the documents back and keeping quiet. But if she refused—well, I don't think he would have let her get away."

"How did Banner kidnap you, though?" Bess asked Toby.

"He arrested me," Toby said. "Then he drove me out of town. And the rest—the struggle in the car, my escape—you know."

"Hey, what's going on here?"

The girls looked up to see Donald Wood and Arthur Ferranti approaching the cabin. "Are you celebrating?" Wood asked.

"Can we join you?" Ferranti sat down. "How's your head, Toby? Feeling better?"

"Wonderful," Toby said. "No more headaches. I feel like a new person."

"You look it, too," Nancy said with a smile. "Have some lemonade, all of you."

"We were just discussing the case," Bess said.

She blushed slightly as the red-haired Ferranti sat down beside her. "And I have a question to ask you. How did you end up in the woods on our first day here—scaring a poor city girl like me half to death?"

"I guess you do deserve an explanation," Ferranti said with a grin. "Toby and Donald were supposed to meet at the Boat Yard Café that afternoon to go over his story. I went to pick Toby up, and I saw her leave in Richard Banner's car. I followed them, but my old car broke down. He got ahead, and I lost him." He frowned. "Not hard to believe if you've seen his snazzy car."

148

Ferranti accepted a glass of lemonade from Nancy.

"By the time I caught up with them, Banner's car had already crashed into the tree," he said. "Toby had disappeared. So I went looking for her in the woods."

"Is that how you ended up outside our bathroom window, too?" George asked.

Ferranti nodded. "Donald went to look for Toby, too," he added. "His face got scratched in the woods."

"Dumb branches," Donald remarked.

"And when I saw the two of them sneaking onto the Castles' estate, they were searching for Toby," Nancy finished.

George shook her head. "I'm still confused. What about the message with the rock, and the van driver who practically leveled you in the parking lot? Was that all Banner's work?"

"Yep," said Nancy. "On Mayor Castle's orders, of course."

Bess gave a big sigh and stood up. "And now," she said, "anyone for a celebration swim? Solving mysteries gives me extra energy. We might as well take advantage of it while it lasts."

"Do you feel up to it, Toby?" Nancy asked. "I have an extra swimsuit I can lend you."

"That's exactly what I feel up to," Toby said,

beaming. "You have no idea what a relief it is to feel like a normal person for a change!"

"Oh, yes, we do," George murmured, raising her eyebrows comically at Nancy. "We most certainly do."

Arthur Ferranti and Donald Wood decided to drive back to Minosha for their swim trunks. They promised to rejoin the girls in half an hour.

The girls changed into their bathing suits and headed down to the dock. On the way, George said, "One more detail, Nan. Who phoned Donald Wood when you were hiding in his closet? Was it Arthur Ferranti?"

"Exactly," Nancy said. "He'd done some extra research and needed another look at the documents."

"I've got a question, too." Bess hurried to keep up with them. "Why was Donald talking to the mayor in Town Hall? When the mayor said he'd like to get rid of people playing detective?"

"Oh, yes." Nancy laughed. "The mayor was talking about Donald. Donald tried to interview Castle, to add some balance to his article. But Castle wouldn't have anything to do with him. Donald said he was very rude."

"Nothing like solving a perfect puzzle," Bess sang. She walked out on the dock and prepared

to dive. "All the little pieces in place. I love it."
An instant later she was in the water.

The girls swam for a while. Then they floated
on their backs while they talked about the rest
of their vacation.

"I guess this is our chance to go to the
theater and to really check out the shops in
Minosha," Nancy said.

"Not me," Bess announced. She paddled
with her feet a few times. "I'm staying right
here. No more civilization for me. I'm even
going to try out the water skis."

"How long do you think she'll keep this up?"
Nancy asked George.

"Depends on how many bags of taco chips
are left," George answered. All the girls gig-
gled.

It seemed like no time before they heard
Donald Wood's voice coming from the path.

"We did it!" he yelled.

He and Arthur Ferranti appeared, in their
swim trunks with towels slung around their
shoulders. Wood carried a sack of newspapers
under one arm.

"Take a look at this," Wood said. He handed
out copies of the newspaper.

It was a special edition of the *Minosha Daily
News.*

151

" 'Paper Mill Fraud Revealed.' " Nancy read the largest headline aloud.

" 'Mayor Castle Under Investigation.' " Toby read another headline.

"There's going to be a press conference tonight," Ferranti said. "We've all got to be there."

"I'm afraid your vacation is going to be disturbed again," Toby apologized. "But I hope you won't be involved after tonight."

"What time's the press conference?" Bess asked quickly. She was pulling on her sandals and gathering up her towel.

"Uh-oh," Nancy said, laughing. "Will she have time to wash her hair and do her nails?"

"That's not the problem." Bess hurried toward the path. "I've got to drive into Minosha to find that white dress."

She turned back to look at everyone on the dock for just a moment. "You know, sometimes you just can't escape civilization!"